Zhang Legacy

ALSO BY WENDY COTTIERS

Mischa and Benji: The Feline Royalty of Tuna Island

Cottiers Photography Golden Sky

Kismet- a Novellete

Healthy is not a Size, it is a Lifestyle: Living GMO Free in the 21st Century

Positive Nut

The Bare Truth GMO-Free Diet

Buon Appetito: Family Recipes

RAVES FOR ZHANG LEGACY

"I fall in love with Wendy's **MAGICAL** gem of characters, even the backstabbing ones. They took me on a **WILD** and **WONDERFUL** trip. Looking forward to the sequel." - Cathryn Konners, U.S. Air Marshal

"Great Story! Drew me in and kept me coming back. An **EXCELLENT** tale of two friends." - Nick

"I **LOVE** this book. It keeps me on the edge of my seat. Something different. Most of all I love the pages and how it's easy to read. Can't wait for the next one." - Kelly

"Outstanding. I **HIGHLY** recommend it! Must READ -You will NOT be disappointed! The Book Kept Me Intrigued. I'm looking forward to reading the sequel Infinity and other novels from this Author!" - Cheryl

"Good writer, book was so **GOOD** I bought one for a friend …. Now waiting for the audio to come out." - Mark

"Your novel seems to be in **PERFECT TIMING** with our world now!! Genius." - Eric

Zhang Legacy Trilogy

A Novel

by WENDY COTTIERS

AUDIOBOOK NARRATED BY

Niall Semple

Written in 10 Languages

The characters and events in this book are fictitious. Any similarity to real persons, living or dead, is coincidental and not intended by the author.

Copyright © 2021 by Wendy Cottiers

Cover design by Francine Jacobson.

All rights reserved.

Information about permission to reproduce selections from this book, write to trade permissions@pp.com or wendycottiers@att.net

First Edition

10 2021

ISBN: 9798498006574

Printed in the United States of America

1. Fiction 2. Sci-Fi 3. Romance 4. Novel   Cottiers, Wendy.

TO RYDER

Thanks for the story

TABLE OF CONTENTS

CHAPTER 1 ZHANG'S 1

CHAPTER 2 INFINITY 23

CHAPTER 3 PALM BEACH PREP 44

CHAPTER 4 TALE OF TWO 64

CHAPTER 5 GARNET'S LETTER 93

CHAPTER 6 KARMA 114

CHAPTER 7 OLD FRIEND'S 129

CHAPTER 8 VICTORIAS' VISIONS 143

CHAPTER 9 PLUS, ONE 151

CHAPTER 10 REBOUND 170

CHAPTER 11 BLACK SHEEP 191

CHAPTER 12 CASH ZHANG 203

CHAPTER 13 VICTORIA DEROSSI 211

CHAPTER 14 ZHANG FAMILY HOLDINGS 224

CHAPTER 15 MARKET PLUMMETS 235

CHAPTER 16 BADASS BITCHES 243

CHAPTER 17 WEDDING BLISS 259

CHAPTER 18 MCADAMS 272

CHAPTER 19 DISCOVERY 283

CHAPTER 20 TO THOSE WHO COME & GO 299

CHAPTER 21 REINCARNATION 308

CHAPTER 22 FRUITION 316

CHAPTER 23 SPACE EXPEDITIONS 330

CHAPTER 24 THE DEPOPULAITON AGENDA 339

CHAPTER 25 CORONAVIRUS HELL 2030 348

CHAPTER 26 MYSTERIES OF THE ZHANG LEGACY 355

CHAPTER 27 SILENT SIGNALS 360

CHAPTER 28 THE 3-0161 GENE EXPERIMENT 377

ABOUT THE AUTHOR 389

ZHANG LEGACY

CHAPTER 1
ZHANG'S

Zenya awoke to the faint sounds of Mozart's *Fantasia in D minor, K.397*, feeling slightly hypnopompic, yet still able to recall her heart-racing dream long enough to put it to paper. The dreams varied in nature, ranging from black-and-white scenes to vibrant colors, including three-dimensional imagery with objects, landscapes, tsunamis, earthquakes, and death and destruction. She also experienced the eerie sensation of déjà vu, vivid memories of loved ones' faces, and encounters with people she had never met before.

At times, she felt as though she were the only one in her family experiencing these sensory phenomena, caught in an almost half-dream state. Every morning, she religiously wrote in one of her three journals. She lived and breathed these journals, o often storing them in her bedroom safe or tucking them away beneath the mattress pad. The blue journal documented every dream she could remember upon waking. The cover of the pink poem notebook featured an image of the heroine Usagi Tsukino and her Sailor Guardians, battling to protect the world from all manner of supernatural evil.

Her prized yellow journal contained stories about the family, infused with humor and wit. That cover was labeled ("S A T I R E S C R E E N - P L A Y") Zenya uses irony and exaggeration to criticize people, corporations, government, and society. The purpose of the satire was to make the reader laugh, and this journal was a compilation of things she overheard her father mainly discussing around the dinner table. She jumped from the Marie Antoinette antique white daybed, landing one foot on a fluffy white rug as she reached for her Zhang-logo bathrobe. She was excited because today Grandma would be arriving. During Garnet's last visit in September, when she brought a luxurious ivory baby mink hooded coat, she purchased it for Zenya while attending the New York Fashion Show. Longtime friend and fashion designer Sergio custom-made it for Zenya to match Garnet's mink. A sophisticated addition to any little girl's wardrobe.

At the bottom of the closet sat a fingerprint-reading lock. Zenya placed her finger on the reader, unlocking the safe. Each bedroom in the estate was equipped with a custom-made lock crafted from solid aerospace-grade aluminum, designed exclusively for the Zhang family. She retrieved the blue journal, closed the safe, and sat at the Marie Antoinette–crafted desk to write about her dream.

With a steady hand, she penned in black ink: *"To Those Who Come & Go."* It was the same recurring tsunami dream she had since she was in her mother's womb. The kind that wakes you up in the middle of a deep sleep: an eerie dream of death, destruction, and a Xian Warrior. One might call it a nightmarish dream, but the little girl wanted to return to it night after night to see her hero—the warrior hero. She ended her morning writing with, "Looking up at the sky is looking back in time. The further away we look, the further back in time we peer into the history of the universe."

Zenya showered, dressing in her school uniform: a plaid skirt and a white button-down shirt with the school crest. Her bedroom lay at the very end of the corridor. The stacked books on her nightstand ranged from a collection of works by George Orwell, P.D. Ouspensky, Edgar Allan Poe, Beethoven, Wagner, Dali, Carl Jung, Tesla, Nostradamus, and many more. Zenya ran to the French door, which had eight panes of glass. As she opened her bedroom door, she could see her sister's reflection.

"Stop spying on me, you ugly brat," said Chia, who was staring at herself in the mirror as she put pink lip gloss on. "I know you are, but what am I?" Zenya said, convincing herself she was smarter.

Chia was eight years older, a real tormentor most of the time. She resented babysitting Zenya when no help was around, which ultimately made her the most mischievous sibling. Pushing her out of the way, as if the girls were in the middle of a playground or after-school taunt, Chia shouted, "Bet you five bucks I'll beat you to the kitchen, you little brat."

The rollicking laughter from the girls echoed throughout the second floor of the large home. From Cash's bedroom came the noises of thump, thump, thump, woof, woof, roof, bark, ruff, and scratching at the back of the door.

"Hey, stop running! Sundance wants out," the boy yelled while opening the door ajar, trying to calm the Siberian Husky. The exterior of his bedroom door had a "Do Not Enter" sign hanging. On the back of the door was an autographed poster of his imaginary girlfriend, the beautiful Morgan Fairchild, and he kissed it nightly, wishing her sweet dreams.

His parents had gifted him a one-year-old trained purebred dog for his birthday. Sundance often slept at the edge of his bed in his super cool airplane-themed bedroom.

The room had a navy color scheme, and the ceiling and mural walls were painted by the famous artist Jada Zoo. A unique airplane-shaped bed filled the middle of the room, made from an aluminum frame. Cloud-filled sky, map-print bedding, and airplane toys filled the space. Two authentic World War II fighter-plane-inspired chairs sat beside the aluminum aviator-wing desk, adjacent to the floor-to-ceiling window, giving the room a decidedly aerodynamic feel. The parents were under the impression that a well-themed bedroom would further influence his behavior and views on life.

Zhang's seven-bedroom home sits on 8,808 square feet within the super-exclusive Victoria Peak. Security is tight in this affluent neighborhood, as it sits at an elevation of 1,811 feet, the highest point on Hong Kong Island. Two terra-cotta warriors perched on the tallest staircase, one in each corner, as you enter the home through the grand foyer. Zhang's close-knit family of six is known for their decorated personalities. The house had just enough space for the children to have privacy away from one another. The children's bedrooms each had a secret door connected to the underground panic room, which the parents called a secret hiding place.

Mai Kai Lee has brown hair pulled back in a ponytail, dressed in a white Gucci button-down shirt with the Zhang crescent, a black skirt, and a black apron. She is making the typical Asian breakfast, including steamed buns, pork dumplings, crullers, and warm bowls of congee (Chinese rice porridge), or zhou, a bowl of watery rice that resembles porridge. Crullers, twisted strips of deep-fried dough, are the food of choice to serve with congee. Yuan is dipping his cruller into the congee and watching the news.

"Good morning, Nanny Mai Kai. I will eat my congee in the library," yelled the charismatic Zenya as she skipped down the corridor, joyfully shouting that, once again, she had beaten Chia.

Mai Kai has been a proud employee of the Zhang family for over fifty years. Garnet and Xian hired her husband, Sanjay, as an Estate Manager to oversee multiple Zhang residences. Yuan thought of Mai Kai as his second mother. When Sanjay passed, Garnet insisted that it was time for Mai Kai to move into the Hong Kong Estate. Coincidentally, it was the same year Amida was born. Yuan was only 23, and the additional help for his new bride would be appreciated. Mai Kai welcomed the offer, moving into the beautiful estate home. Her other duties include overseeing the estate's housekeeping and maintenance staff. The gardeners deal directly with the lady of the house. The lush green lawn and landscaping are impeccable, surrounding the pool area with dense woods just off Pollock's Path, which claims the title of the world's most expensive street.

Zenya extended her hand, high-fiving her whistling father as she zoomed by him into the library. She planted herself into the reclining brown leather chair next to him.

"Today is the first day of spring," Zenya said quietly.

"You are brilliant, my little jellybean," said Yuan, a handsome man with sunken cheeks and stringy black hair. He was looking out over the harbor while watching the countdown to the 9:00 a.m. opening bell of the Hong Kong market, the fourth-largest stock market in the world.

Yuan, sipping a cup of green tea and exchanging greetings with Mai Kai Lee as she handed a glass of fresh-squeezed orange juice to Zenya, who had her favorite neon-colored pink crazy straw and a gummy vitamin placed on the folded Zhang-engraved napkin.

"Daddy, why don't you ever share a cup of juice with me?" Zenya asked, looking genuinely shocked, remembering that Garnet loved juice in the morning.

Yuan thought for a second. "Green tea contains catechins that help prevent computer radiation and supplement the moisture content of the human body," he said.

"Awesome, whatever that means," Zenya said with great excitement.

On days Zenya made it down before her siblings, she would sit quietly reading *Nostradamus*, fascinated by his 21st-century prophecies of events such as tsunamis and outbreaks of diseases. They would play a game called Zhang decisions, which was taught to him by his great-grandfather Xian when he was a small boy. Most days, Yuan would arrive in the estate's library to catch up on emails and plan his day. Zenya chose the bag with a hundred ten-cent American coins totaling $10.00 USD or 100 Hong Kong dollars. Arithmetic is her favorite field of study, knowing it was a $2.90 USD profit by picking the Hong Kong dollars every time.

"Come here, my little jellybean, and give your old man a hug," Yuan said. It was then he whispered in her ear to invest it wisely as he handed her 100 HKD. "Next time, we will play with the Iranian Rial to see how smart you really are," Yuan said as he hugged her tightly.

Before any socializing was allowed, the children *must* study English for one hour. In the evenings, the four siblings—Amida, Chia, Zenya, and Cash—were allowed to stay in their pajamas while sipping green tea in the study. Zenya would sit quietly in the corner, looking out the window while watching her father read a book or sit at the Steinway concert grand piano. The children would often share a laugh while reading the obituaries, each pondering their legacy. Yuan created a game where each child had to imagine their own story of contributing to society. The winner would receive one thousand shares in the family stock. To date, there had only been two ties between Zenya and Chia.

Maybe this is where the resentment started, because Zenya was a natural at that game, their father would say. Not only did she exemplify strength in her poised mannerisms, but also in her speech. An immediate representation shows the young girl's bravery, passion, and determination to constantly challenge herself to be the best—eight and wise beyond her years. Zenya is the youngest of the children by several minutes, as she and Cash are fraternal twins, yet she is strikingly taller, has a thinner frame, deep green eyes, and straight black shoulder-length hair.

All four siblings have lived in the estate home since birth. It was indeed a double blessing for Yuan, who was shocked when his wife announced they were having twins—also double the trouble.

Cash entered the study, saying, "Dad, I liked your Symphony No. 41, Jupiter piece."

Yuan smiled, thrilled that he could even name a Mozart piece. Out of all the children, Cash was the most popular in school, and all the girls loved his upbeat, friendly demeanor. Yuan knew it wouldn't be long before he'd have to discuss the birds and the bees, but he understood that everything had its time.

"Welcome, Cash, and good morning, my athletic prodigy son, Amida. Cash, that was *Fantasia in D minor*. One day, you'll learn how to play and impress the ladies. Now, boys, sit down and eat your breakfast while it's still hot. Would you like anything else from Mai Kai?" Yuan asked, his tone filled with genuine interest.

"I'm not hungry. Plus, I have a karate lesson later today, and I prefer to have an empty stomach," said Amida. "Beautiful Nanny Mai Kai, please wrap it up. I'd rather eat my breakfast in the car," said Cash. "Ask your father, please," said Mai Kai Lee. The stubborn boy refused, grabbing his book bag in a hurry. "That's fine, Mai Kai," said Yuan, winking at her as he wrapped his arms around his children in a group hug.

"Dad, I am driving myself to school today," Chia said confidently.

"Oh no, you are not driving; you go with Benji as usual," Yuan said.

"Segway cop, you mean, right, Dad?" Chia asked, rolling her eyes at him.

"Zu mu and Wai gong will be eagerly awaiting your arrival. They will be here this afternoon and will be joining us for 晚餐 (Wǎncān). Children, I ask you, please be on your best behavior, and do not ask Wai gong Xian about his recent surgery unless he brings it up," Yuan said as he peeked out the window, watching his flirty wife speaking with the gardener— a little closer than he expected. Hoping not another fling?Amida, 17, looked up at the sky. He is the oldest of all the children and the first to reach the awaiting driver. The teenager was quiet today, scrolling through Facebook on his new iPhone. He noticed symptoms of depression and anxiety but wouldn't dare tell his parents for fear of having the same diagnosis as

Aurora. The rest of the siblings piled into the black-armored, bulletproof Mercedes-Benz S600 Sedan. Benji was the family's chauffeur and security for over five years. Former UK Police and ex-military, Benji dressed in a black blazer and t-shirt underneath a tactical bulletproof vest.

The children's mother, Aurora, has beautiful skin with a medium brown color and golden undertones. She slowly walks to the car, knocking on the window. Benji rolled down his window, saying nothing as he stared ahead.

"Amida, did you apologize to your father?" Aurora asked, smiling with a condescending tone.

"Chia rolled her eyes at Amida while she sent a text to her friend about tonight's party. Cash refused to chime in as he sat patiently, his left hand in his cache shorts pocket, touching the lucky rabbit foot keychain that Grandmother Garnet had given him."

"Cash, what is in your pocket?" Chia asked. In her witticism voice, Chia said to him, "You know what they say: depends on the foot of a rabbit, if you will; just remember, it did not work for that rabbit in your pocket."

Aurora wears a sleeveless white silk top with a blinding emerald necklace around her neck, a light pink ballerina skirt, and white Prada tennis shoes. Her angry face appeared to be sending out daggers, with one hand rolling her platinum-white manicured fingers through her short blonde hair and the other hand resting on her hip.

"Amida, answer me," said Aurora.

"No, Aurora, I am not apologizing. The other boy in school started the fight this time. Father is crazy to punish me again; I am eighteen years old," said Amida.

"It is *Mom*, not Aurora, and you are only seventeen, Amida. You must show me some respect, or you will be grounded for another week," Aurora said.

Amida rolls up the window, signaling to Benji that it is time to leave. Aurora turns away from the car, disgusted by her son Amida's immature behavior.

"You know your father is only looking out for your well-being. Trust me, it is not about the color of the belt, but the self-defense skills learned," said Benji.

"When I was twelve, he grounded me for an after-school fight and for not passing my black belt test when I was sixteen. I gave it my all; that test consisted of five hours of technique and drills. It is ridiculous; it is impossible to live up to his expectations. I can't wait to go to college and move out of this house," Amida said.

"You must come to meditation training with me and let off that steam. You are too young to have this much anger," Benji said.

"I prefer you drive and not talk," Amida said. "Can you drive any slower?" Chia asked. "What do you think Grandma Garnet will bring us?" Zenya asked. None of the children commented. Benji noticed the siblings were ignoring sweet Zenya.

"Something spectacular," Benji said.

They reached school without any arguments. Benji got out of the car and opened the SUV door. Amida slid across the seat, and a Magnum Trojan XL condom fell out of his pocket. Benji just shook his head. Amida winked at Benji while picking it up from the backseat. Turning back, Chia said, "Bye, Segway. Don't kill anyone today."

Aurora acted awkwardly as she entered the estate home, removing her tennis shoes at the front door. "What were you talking to Javier about?" Yuan asked. "The caterpillars in the Yoshino cherry trees," Aurora said as she walked slowly to the door.

"I figured you were discussing the details of our annual cherry blossom party with Javier," Yuan said. "What time will my monster-in-law, Garnet, be here?" Aurora asked as she thought of the last time they were together.

"Does it matter? Just please have everything set up if they want to stay the weekend with the kids, and call her mom or zǔ mǔ," Yuan said. His bride never liked Garnet, and she was already anxious about her arrival. Aurora had been pregnant with Amida at 21 years old. Her mother was upset, saying she was too young. In hindsight, Aurora would have married filmmaker Samuel. Although they lost touch, she often read about him making headlines, particularly when he was the first to discover the SS *Mauriello*, a 470-foot-long 1940s shipwreck just west of Lamma Island. The ship was formerly a luxury cruise ship, converted in 1970 into a Sino-Japanese warship. It is upright at 120 feet below the surface at its deepest.

CHAPTER 2

INFINITY

"It's 3:45 pm, Friday, and Benji is patiently sitting inside the family's SUV, awaiting the arrival of the Zhang clan. For the most part, they had been a low-key family. There had only been one kidnapping threat this year, which ended up being a prank from an upset ex-girlfriend. Sari was one year older than Amida and had attended the same preparatory school, dumping him earlier in the year. When he started to help at his father's investment firm, he realized she was not the girl for him. Sari called the family, saying Amida was not at school, and found a disturbing ransom note in his school locker. Yuan agreed not to press charges. They kept it private and out of the local Hong Kong papers, which would have gone viral if it had reached the media. The family's lawyer insisted the girl sign a non-disclosure agreement.

The usual lineup of black limos, sedans, armored bodyguards, and men dressed in black suits and dark shades awaited Hong Kong's future elite of the world. Scary, Benji thought, as he waved two fingers to a passing driver. The special ops reached out to Benji three years ago for his help in capturing Mahalek Sinsterie, who had strong ties with the Afghanistan underground money-laundering and drug ring. It was called Project A-l-e-c. The family wouldn't allow him to leave unless he had two replacements on call.

With endless headlines about the family's fortune, it was a vulnerable time for the Zhang family as reporters flocked near the home. A recent photo in the newspaper titled, "Zhang's Wealth Soars to Infinity," captured a photograph of the Zhang family standing with the 2,000-year-old warrior at the

Museum's Annual Gala. It was a fundraiser held annually to support the works of the family's legacy. According to the FBI, the family's Terracotta Army Warrior is estimated to be worth US$4.5 million.

That was the same week Aurora reported that her canary diamond engagement ring went missing, and she believed it was at the bottom of the indoor pool. Retired FBI Agent Jack Woods came to protect the family. Aurora was busted for having sex with Jack. Rumor has it that Yuan walked in on them, punching him in the face and then walking away. From that moment, Benji made a pact that he would never leave the family alone again. Benji would have liked to see the look on Yuan's face. It must have taken some self-control not to continue kicking Jack's ass. A disciplined black belt, Yuan decided a punch was terrible enough but well deserved, as Jack was a real asshole.

Aurora calling Benji seemed wildly out of the ordinary. The iPhone rang. At the other end of the phone was a nasty voice. "The devil-in-law, Garnet, is here. Drive faster, and where are my kids?" Aurora asked.

Chia was the first to arrive, opening the back door as she helped Zenya step into the SUV. Amida and Cash jumped in a second later. "Yes, ma'am, we are en route and arriving at 16:15," Benji said. On the other end, the click sounds of dead air, not even a goodbye from high-strung Aurora. Not his business, but he secretly hoped she took her medication today with water and not vodka. As they pulled up into the gated driveway, in the distance, Yuan and Grandfather Xian could be seen practicing Chinese Kung Fu, which is more of a holistic family tradition than self-defense. All the men in the family were black belts and had taken classes at China's 河南登封塔沟少林武术学校 (Henan Dengfeng Shaolin Martial Arts School), which was a famous martial arts school founded in 1914.

Zenya, almost falling out of the car as she couldn't get out faster, ran to Grandmother Garnet, sitting in a white iron chair in the shade while watching the men practice. It was a humid day in May, and the clocks were striking at half-past four. Sundance stretched out on the artificial turf. The dog's cedar gazebo-style kennel has indoor and outdoor comforts, including an electric fan, stainless steel bowls for organic, non-GMO dog food, and purified water. Garnet's gigantic white and green flowered straw hat flew in the wind. Zenya chased it, brought it back, placed it softly on her grandmother's head, and hugged her from the back. Grandmother zǔ mǔ has dark brown, shoulder-length hair with gray streaks, fashionably dressed in a short-sleeve St. John ivory jacket with a metallic green knit pencil skirt.

Arching one brow, Garnet asked, "Zenya, why did you not greet your mother? Is everything all right between you two?"

Aurora shook her head, looking over at Javier working in the garden, trying her hardest to keep calm while ignoring her mother-in-law's backhanded comment. Garnet surmised that something must be wrong.

"Of course, everything is perfect between my daughter and me," Aurora said.

"Too many kids show worrying signs of fragility from a very young age, blaming parents for their anxiety disorder," said Garnet.

Whenever Garnet came to visit the family, it was often a time that Aurora felt ignored, sometimes even blindsided, as it was apparent that the children truly loved spending time with her.

Garnet, protective over her only son Yuan, wondered what Aurora was up to now. What had she been staring at just beyond the cherry blossoms? Garnet assumed she had been having an affair, but she was unsure with whom.

Stanley Jordan's *The Lady in My Life* played from the outside Bose speakers. Mai Kai Lee brought out pineapple buns with a fresh pot of oolong tea as she knew the men would need to quench their thirst. The men were not as talkative and raucous as the ladies but silent, sullen, and vindictive.

Yuan greeted his mother, Garnet. "Neih hou (pronounced 'nay-ho,' which is how they say hello when in Hong Kong) to the best lady in my life," Yuan said.

Garnet eyed him affectionately, infected by the boisterous gladness of his mood. They were praying that Aurora was not upsetting him again.

Wai Xian approached them as he wiped the sweat from his forehead with a monogrammed Zhang-embroidered handkerchief. Wai Xian reached out with a handshake accompanied by a nod and direct eye contact. "Aurora, my lovely daughter-in-law, you look well-rested," Xian said.

"How are you enjoying being an inhabitant of the filthy Billionaires' Row?" Aurora joked.

"Well, with a block of our wealthy friends living in the adjacent skyscrapers in the Big Apple, we tend to feel as if we are still in Tokyo," Xian said.

"You both should visit more often," Garnet said. "We will make a plan just as soon as we see those Northern Lights," Yuan said.

Aurora would complain, stating that her husband does not put family first. That was an inside joke between them. He would often promise, in the slow season, next year, when Aurora would ask to take a vacation alone, leaving the children with Mai Kai.

"We had to cancel our trip to India last month. Aurora's mother, Madhuri, celebrated her 60th birthday without us," Yuan said.

"When we heard about India's bubonic and pneumonic plague outbreak, we couldn't chance it with the kids. I am even shocked that you flew here," Aurora said.

"Well, dear, the plague is in India, not fabulous NY or Hong Kong. Besides, we were on our Gulfstream, and it was safe. Nothing to worry about, dear. The pilots and our favorite cabin attendant, Priscilla, flew with us. No general public. No masks and no one sneezing on us," said Garnet.

"Shit, it is sobering to stay in the City, and our neighbors are as depressed as the water rats," Xian said.

"That depends on which news media outlet they are watching," Yuan said. He chuckled as Garnet winked at him.

When Grandfather Xian was diagnosed with atherosclerosis, Grandmother insisted they move permanently into their five-bedroom penthouse on NYC's Fifth Avenue. It is stunning, with three stories of fabulous views of Central Park, including a 1,500 square-foot wraparound terrace plus indoor extras like a gym, media room, and library. Throughout the years, they would visit in the winter, periodically frequenting Zhang Hampton's family estate.

The family would fly in from Hong Kong to visit the

grandmother a few times a year, although she and the staff knew it was for lavish parties thrown night after night. Never wanting to return to that house, Grandmother would agree to make the two-hour trip, sometimes even taking the Hampton Jitney, where she would dress down and converse with everyday folks. It was the only time Grandfather would allow Garnet to travel without security. Later, we found out that it was because he would arrange to meet his assistant at the Plaza. They would have a romp in room 808 for over ten years.

Mai Kai Lee rounded up the children, advising them they had fifteen minutes to wash up before dinner. Chia was on her coral Apple iPhone, FaceTiming her boyfriend. Yeung was arrested for driving drunk, which carried a maximum fine of HK$25,000 and imprisonment for three years. His parents could not afford to hire a good lawyer; the courts mandated him to attend a driving improvement course and have his license revoked for six months.

Yeung was grounded for one month, and Chia slowly lost interest as he seemed to distance himself from her at school. Perhaps she was a bad influence on him. Yuan did not like the idea of his first daughter being in the car with Yeung when the cops arrested him. Photos from the shameful evening made it to the local Victoria Peak newspaper.

Yuan and Aurora felt ashamed but knew they could not do anything about it. They often spoke about sending her to a boarding school in America, but they knew she would refuse to leave Yeung.

Michelin-star Lobar Hong Kong Steakhouse's talented Chef Marco arrived earlier to prep the evening meal. Walking into the kitchen, pouring himself a whiskey, Yuan said, "You know, my Wall Street friends say NY Lobar is expensive and to be prepared to have a wallet homicide."

Chef Marco and sous-chef, thirty-one-year-old Sin, agreed. "That is why Aurora organizes these elegant dinner parties. Catering invoices are for her eyes only," said Mai Kai. She was cleaning the crystal glasses using a wine-glass cleaning cloth.

"What's on tonight's menu?" Yuan asked, smiling from ear to ear, looking enthusiastic.

"Steak Tartare with Foie Gras, thick-cut smoked bacon with caramelized onions, bourbon-baked apples, and Australian Wagyu. Truffle Mac & cheese for the children with baked pork chops," Chef Marco said.

The family sits around the Southern Chinese antique dining

room table made from rosewood with bird and flower carvings. Raising his platinum flute of Dom Pérignon, "To health, wealth, and happiness," Yuan said. He is sitting at the head of the table. The younger children were all on their best behavior, sipping colorful mint soda mocktails.

Garnet passes around what appeared to be a thin black book to each Zhang grandchild. It was small, 5 inches tall by 3.5 inches wide, like a passport. The shiny infinity logo sparkled in the light and appeared to be in 3D, engraved on the front. Inside was the child's photograph at birth, including a 24-carat gold-stamped Infinity coin. Engraved on the back of the coins were eight numbers.

Yuan stood up, tapping Chef Marco's shoulder. "1980 was an outstanding year. You know the owner of Lobar is a good friend of Carlos DeRossi, CEO of Carlo's Holdings," Yuan said as he took a sip of his whiskey.

Yuan met resort tycoon Carlos while dining at Lobar a few weeks back. They had many things in common and discussed upcoming mergers and acquisitions, including the Lama Island Resort. But rather than dismantling the company, Yuan proposed that they work together to save it. Yuan would not agree to anything until they took the central ferry at pier 4 to the island. He was similar to Garnet when it came to the general public, as he could see the big picture and the financial gain of investing in the island. Yet, he refused to take the helicopter with Carlos, as he wanted to see how convenient it would be for the ordinary people to travel, especially during New Year celebrations.

While growing up in Asia, Xian never sugar-coated anything in business for his only son. Maybe this prompted Yuan to go into business acquisitions, not his father Xian's influence. Yuan rubbed elbows with the ultra-rich and the blue-collar workers to get a feel for all walks of life. In publications, they called him the wealthy businessman who purchased suffering companies. Along the way, he made a few good friends, unlike his silver-spooned father Xian, who could have lived off his twentieth birthday party money—like what they call a confirmation party in the Catholic religion.

The Zhangs spent the weekend quietly at home. The adults were reminiscing about life in America vs. living in a Marxist-Leninist state, a communist country.

"If the people don't stop it now, your mother and I feel that Marxism will take over the American way of life," Xian said.

"I agree; people can no longer sit and watch or want to be left alone. American Patriots seem fed up," Yuan said.

"It does not affect our family. I don't know why you even bother discussing this," Aurora said.

Garnet nodded her head at her son. "That is the problem right here, in this room. Aurora, we are all affected, regardless of nationality, race, or color. Even wealth should not stand in the way of what is right and fair. When we must head to the underground bunker condominiums, we will not be worried about any of those things. It is about the Lotus Sutra—about nature, humanity, and the righteous laws to live a fair and decent life. To continue our legacy walking within the light of Shintoism," Yuan said.

The twins, Cash and Zenya, were on the second floor, quietly hiding in the corner of the steps, listening to them laugh and tell stories into the wee hours of the night. Zenya had big ears and was trying to hear what they were saying about Infinity, as she couldn't quite grasp what the present was from Nanny Garnet. She would be going to school tomorrow without any fancy stories to share, and they told her not to tell anyone about Infinity, whatever that meant.

Aurora was the first to say goodbye, as she was starting to feel anxious and didn't want to have another nasty spell of vertigo. Yuan knew his parents would be leaving soon to prepare for their long trip back to America.

Yuan slowly walked them out to the front entrance of the estate home. It was time for him to say goodbye.

"Mother, you could have waited to gift the kids with the Infinity card," Yuan said.

Garnet just shrugged her shoulders at him as she looked at Xian to respond.

"Son, it must be now, as the world is too volatile, and we never know what can happen to any of us. We are older now and ready to move on to the next phase of our life. You cannot rely on us to plan the course of the future. Our grandchildren are the last of our legacy. We hope that one day they will have a family of their own. They will each need to reproduce, even if that means on another planet. And, son, they cannot misplace that coin," Xian said.

Garnet smiled at her son and said, "Mai Kai Lee has been instructed to give the children Diamond tea in the morning, as it will help relieve the anxiety of the Infinity coin discussion. Zenya will be reciting every word heard at dinner, perhaps even writing about it. She is a smart girl and too young to understand what a secret means. Please do not give away any answers to her endless questions. Yuan, this must be kept secretive from the world, including her teachers and friends at school."

Yuan was tired of the conversation and ready to find his wife. "Do you understand, Yuan?" Xian asked in disbelief, as his son was not listening to a word he was saying.

Smiling and nodding his head to say yes, yet still baffled, Yuan hugged his parents goodbye. Yuan knew Garnet was up to no good. Could the world be entering the final stages? That dreadful tipping point when it would be time to hibernate in underground bunkers where the wealthy hide from coronavirus with fancy filtration systems in their homes, cars, and private planes? It was the new world's roller coaster ride of what some call the end days.

Their driver, Lumpur, patiently waited with the engine on in the black town car.

Cash and Zenya were peeking out the window, sad that the grandparents were leaving. Before Yuan walked back inside the house, the twins sprinted to each bedroom, quietly closing the door.

As he watched the car pull out of the driveway heading down Victoria Peak, Yuan wondered once again why Garnet gave the children an Infinity coin at such a young age.

Typically, the flight from Hong Kong to New York spans sixteen hours, but aboard Garnet's $150 million Gulfstream G650ER, renowned for its superior cruising speeds, the journey is completed in under fourteen hours. With its exceptional range, this jet effortlessly covers vast distances in less time. Upon arrival at Teterboro Airport, the tarmac is lined with an exclusive fleet of limousines, awaiting the arrival of jets returning from the weekend.

CHAPTER 3

PALM BEACH PREP

Victoria missed school in Hong Kong, where her classmates were drama-free, much brighter, made better daily choices, and partied less. Victoria had lived in Palm Beach long enough to appreciate her close friends while knowing the backstabbers, but nobody had been a better friend than Zenya. The valedictorian, soon-to-be criminal attorney, gave the graduating students this caveat: stay in the far-right lane if you are drunk and driving under the speed limit.

On graduation night, the friends partied at the Breakers Resort until 2 a.m. Victoria was happy that Carlos had reserved the presidential floor with ten oceanfront rooms for her and the girls' dates to enjoy. Carlos sent a text to his daughter earlier in the evening, telling her to be safe and not mix alcohol.

"I am proud of you, and I know you will make the right choice to work for me. I am looking forward to our annual diving trip to Fiji in a few weeks. Please convince Valentina to join us this time. She is your one and only sister, and it bothers me that you do not make time for her. Love you, kid. xo, your father."

Carlos was hoping that she would listen to him and call Valentina. It wasn't often that he had his two daughters in the same room.

Carlos walked into his office and received the mayor's phone call that the panel had deferred Carlos's Holdings application to project architect Commissioner Joyce Abraham. Carlos needed assistance with the demolition and reconstruction of the Palm Beach 4-story home located at 352 Starlight Road. He had the property zoned for a ten-story solar-powered luxury resort, including boat docks and EV charging stations. The neighboring houses were against the proposed building, protesting daily, as it would block their million-dollar ocean views.

Murphy Law Firm, est. 1975, was just a bottom-feeder firm, with Vaughn as a newbie associate who often had a hard time going after the poor, down-and-out schmoe who hadn't a nickel to his name. They were the only sharks chasing behind ambulance trucks on the ritzy avenue.

Vaughn would often use one infamous sentence with his wealthiest clients: "When the proper solution can be found, anything can be done. It's always a question of how much money it would take."

Today, they have the best top-notch criminal defense attorneys in the U.S.

Following in his father's footsteps, Lance graduated from FSU with a law degree. During summer break and holidays, he would return to Palm Beach, rubbing elbows with other white-collar friends and their well-educated parents. It was an unspoken inner-circle bubble, and newcomers were not allowed. Handouts, including shared secretive backhanded deals, were favored only among prestigious families, similar to the Shriners.

Lance's parents had been married for over thirty years and were members of the private beach resort. Vaughn had only one requirement to make an appearance at the law firm. As the only son, he would soon be running the Albany, New York, office. Vaughn wanted him away from his airhead of a girlfriend named Lindsey, and with the partner's six-figure salary dangling over his head, he was sure his son Lance would take the bait.

Lindsey, a Floridian, grew up in Palm Beach, the daughter of well-known attorneys Priscilla and Richard Colbert. While attending Palm Beach Prep School, Lindsey met Victoria. One afternoon after a lunch break, Lindsey entered the girls' bathroom and spotted a new girl smoking a cigarette near the window. Lindsey bummed one off the girl.

"You are my neighbor, aren't you? Don't you have an older sister named Valentina? I thought you were living with your father in Vegas or Hong Kong," asked Lindsey.

Victoria's height is 5 ft 10, perfect for a model. She weighs 58 kg (127 pounds) and is a blonde with straight hair, cut shoulder-length in an angled bob. While the girls gossiped and talked about the football players, Donna walked into the room, pushing Victoria and cornering her into a small, dark area. Lindsey and Donna were popular kids in school, and Victoria, a loner, was dropped off at school in a limo.

Victoria didn't have many friends because she had spent the last two years at Hong Kong Prep School. She spent most of her summers traveling with Zenya, vacationing at her father's resorts, or spending time in the Hamptons at Garnet's house.

Donna walked in with such an attitude; she was fearless. An obnoxious bully to Victoria because she had heard that Victoria made fun of David.

"What is your problem, Victoria? You walk around here as if you own the place. You are not in Vegas anymore. This school isn't one of your father's resorts where you can pretend to play the boss's snotty-ass daughter. We don't work for you. You haven't spoken to any of us since you have been back, and now I hear you have been scuzzy to my brother, calling him little. Why are you such a stuck-up Barbie brat?" Asked Donna.

"What are you even saying? David sits behind me and constantly torments me, touching my elbows and telling me to use more lotion while he kicks the back of my chair. He is immature and flies spitballs through a straw across the room to the teacher's back. Class clown and not that funny. Now would you please stop the name-calling?" Victoria said.

Donna towered over Victoria in her three-inch black army boots. She found it funny to make fun of her calling her Barbie all the time behind her back. Donna's father is the city mayor, which explains why she has such an attitude.

"You are either stupid or dumb to think I will believe you. Your dad kisses my father's ass the same way you will," said Donna.   "Listen, you are the one being a brat, and I am not stupid," Victoria said.

Laughing loudly, Donna smiled, saying, "Okay, then you are a dumb ass Victoria."

Lindsey walked closer to Donna, looking at her with her hands waving in the air. "Victoria is my friend. Why can't we all be friends?" Asked Lindsey.

At that very moment, the bathroom fire alarm went off. They laughed, grabbed each other's hands, and ran to the hallway before the school staff could blame them.

After that day, Donna respected Victoria for speaking up even if she was a Barbie, and she realized she wasn't a brat. The truth was that the kids in the class were awful to her because she was the newest kid with a powerful father.

Victoria missed her best friend Zenya, wishing she were back in Hong Kong. The kids in America were different; sometimes, it felt like they were competitive with her. She often forgot that she was well-educated, had traveled more than most of her classmates, and not all the kids came from such a well-connected family as hers. After that day in the girls' bathroom, she and Lindsey became close friends. They were on the graduation committee and planned senior prom at the Breakers Resort.

The most popular girl in school was throwing a graduation bash at her family's Palm Beach estate. Izabella Stephano's comfortable lifestyle—prep schools, homes in Nantucket and Westchester, and a long line of descendants from the same area—made people label her a WASP. Bella was known to have the best parties in school, and her birthday celebrations included stylish excursions to Mykonos and Ibiza with her besties. Victoria's father, Carlos, was friendly with Bella's father, often seen golfing at Mar-a-Lago. Her father was casino-and-resort magnate Wendell Stephano of the Atlantic City Casino and Resorts.

To some extent, some would say he was competition for Carlos Holdings, yet they were two very different players in the travel industry. Carlos Holdings was a global empire, whereas Wendell's properties were more celebrity-driven and only a domestic USA chain. His home, 6,750 square feet, was situated not far from Mar-a-Lago on Billionaire's Row. About an hour's drive south on A1A, you could find Millionaire Mile, but nothing beats the estate homes on the Palm Beach coastline.

Victoria showed up as a third wheel to the party with Lance and Lindsey. The smell of booze filled the air. Shared drugs passed around the living room on serving trays. Victoria never did hard drugs, and she barely ever drank—only the occasional shared joint with Lindsey. She didn't like being around people who let their guard down and drank until they puked but tonight would take a different turn. Bella's uncle Daniel was seen in the corner flirting with Victoria. They spoke about her father's business and what she would do now that high school had ended. He was a mixologist at the swanky, hype bar up the road, frequented by the locals.

"Try one of my cocktails, Victoria," Daniel asked.

"No, that's okay. I don't want anything," Victoria replied.

"You don't trust me? This is the most popular drink at Buddha-Bar. I'll make you a non-alcoholic one then. How about it?" Daniel asked.

Victoria nodded her head, as if to say yes.

The recipe called for two parts white wine mixed with champagne and one part watermelon. Handing her the glass, Daniel smiled as she thanked him while taking a sip. Victoria turned her back for a moment, distracted by the fireworks. Within a few seconds, she began to feel nauseous and appeared pale and faint. She walked up a flight of stairs to Bella's bedroom. *Thank God no one's in bed,* she thought to herself as she ran to the bathroom, lifting the toilet seat. Sweating and shivering, she puked. Victoria was now alone on the bathroom floor, unconscious.

A few hours later, the young girl woke up with tubes up her nose, smelling like vomit. As she opened her eyes, two police officers stood over her bed.

"Have you taken any drugs this evening?" asked Sheriff Diggs.

Touching her neck and glancing down at her arm, she noticed her brand new Tahitian Daytona Mother of Pearl Gold Diamond Rolex was no longer on her left wrist.

"Where is my jewelry?" Victoria asked.

The second cop rephrased the question. "Did anyone give you drugs tonight, Victoria?" he asked, a handsome young rookie on the job. Sheriff Diggs reached over and shook a plastic Ziploc bag in her face. "Is this the Rolex you're sweating over?" he asked, thinking it was worth half his salary.

Smiling and taking a deep breath, Victoria could now focus on the room and her surroundings.

"No, I don't do drugs. I was at a friend's party. Her uncle gave me a drink. The next thing you know, I was hugging the toilet. I think that fancy toilet even had a UV light because my hand felt warm, which is all I remember," Victoria answered.

"This is about a $60,000 watch. Do you remember that?" Sheriff Diggs sarcastically asked.

"We called your father. He's waiting in the lobby. Can you tell us anything else about tonight?" asked the nasty sheriff.

"Not really," said Victoria.

The cops left the room, saying, "Never sit your drink on a counter and turn your back. It's a common thing these days.

Date rape could have happened here this evening. Consider yourself one of the lucky ones," Sheriff Diggs said.

Carlos entered the room as the door swung open. Standing beside her, he said, "Honey, you cannot mix alcohol."

"But I didn't know, Dad, and I wasn't even drinking tonight, I swear," Victoria said.

"Well, you had your stomach pumped and almost died. If Bella's parents hadn't come home in time, I don't know what might have happened to you," Carlos said as he hugged his daughter tightly, trying not to pull the oxygen tubes from her nose. "How about a dad-daughter day on Worth Avenue when you feel better?" Carlos asked.

"Yes, it's a date, Dad," said Victoria.

A middle-aged nurse walked in and said she could leave the hospital after Dr. Phil Yates met with Carlos.

Her wrist was throbbing and severely bruised. All she could think of was the damn cancerous UV light. Victoria reached for her Hermès handbag, pulling out a pink sweater to wear home."

Glancing at her phone, she saw about 20 missed messages from Lindsey.

Text 1: Bella's parents are worried your father will sue them because you were drinking at their house and are underage!

Text 2: Bella's best friend Amy was having sex ☹ in the primary suite with three guys from the swim team. What a slut!

Text 3: Are you okay, girl?

Text 4: I texted Zenya. She was worried about you.

Text 5: I hope you feel better. Call me.

Text 6: Oh, damn it. Carlos just called me.

Victoria stopped at that text and replied: "I will be 18 next week. No lawsuits, and I'm fine. XO."

Seasons come and go, similarly to the people in our lives. Graduation came and went in the blink of an eye, leaving us yearning for more. Many schoolmates wanted one more month, while the teachers were ready to start summer break. Keg parties, weekends of binge-drinking while watching Netflix with classmates, endless athletic competitions, and crash studying by pulling all-nighters had all consummated. Bill-paying and grown-up adulting arrived like the last amphibious species to go extinct in the Amazon, marking the end of an era.

The pressure for the kids to do well in school and ace the admission requirements for a prestigious college was now over, as the graduates knew what lay ahead. If you want to get in, the first hurdle is to look at the acceptance rate, which tells you how competitive the school is and how challenging its requirements are.

The teachers advised that the acceptance rate at Harvard is 4.7%, which scared the hell out of most of us. This meant that for every 100 applicants, only five are admitted.

Most of her classmates had apprenticeship jobs at their parents' companies, while others usually went abroad for the summer. Some of them still smoked marijuana and had high alcohol use, and most of Victoria's classmates were experiencing blackouts at least once a month.

As promised, Carlos blocked out time to take Victoria shopping on Worth Avenue a few weeks after graduation. Standing outside the Breakers Resort, Victoria checked the time. Carlos was later than usual, and she wondered if he had forgotten or was blowing her off to take someone else shopping. Victoria had been staying at the resort since graduation night, mostly enjoying the room's silence and the spa's signature ritual baths. Victoria had to decide if she wanted to take her father up on working beside him or if she would move back to Hong Kong and accept the job to work as a television broadcaster at the Bloomberg Stock Exchange.

Carlos pulled into the resort in a black, carbon-fiber-colored Aspark Owl Hypercar. He had several cars, but this was one of his favorites, as it was the world's fastest electric, high-performance car—and he owned it. Yuan had it shipped directly from the Japanese manufacturer, President Yoshida, to Carlos to pique Americans' interest in the EV market. All the guys at Victoria's school wanted to get their hands on all of her father's toys. Their dads all had marvelous cars, but none as exotic as this one-of-a-kind vehicle.

The manager of the Breakers came running out to check it out. The butterfly doors opened as he held Victoria's right hand to help her get into the car.

"Buckle up, kid," said Carlos.

Victoria whispered, "Hi, Dad. I thought you forgot about me. What's with all the flash today? Of all days, why not bring the driver? Where are we going to put the shopping bags?" She thanked the resort manager as she extended her hand, securing her seatbelt as he closed the car door.

"We're not shopping today, Victoria," Carlos said anxiously.

Approaching Starlight Road, he pulled over, holding architectural renderings in his hand, and said, "Well, what do you think of your future home, Victoria? Please accept this lot as a present for your career choice. Stay and live in Florida, take this property and build a home for yourself. Make it even bigger and better—design it the way you want."

Victoria couldn't believe the lengths her father would go to keep her in Florida. "Please don't pressure me. Let me sleep on it," she said.

"Honey, take it. With that 4.48 GPA—especially after retaking the SAT to improve your score to 1600—good job, kid. That was six hours you'll never get back," Carlos replied tersely. The idea that his daughter wouldn't accept his offer was unimaginable.

TALE OF TWO

About two weeks after graduation, Lance proposed to Lindsey. Most of her friends thought she was pregnant. In middle school, Lance was a varsity football linebacker squatting 445 pounds. He was a kid who played every sport, football being his favorite, until that shitty day when he was suspended indefinitely from the varsity team. Coach Riley caught him with a cooler of beer behind the bleachers while making out with one of the cheerleaders.

Lance's nickname back then was "Six" for his picture-perfect six-pack abs. He had a handsome, tanned body with muscular arms, towering at 5'9", dirty blonde wavy hair, brown eyes, and was three years older than Lindsey. The girls were introduced to Lance while working at his father's law firm in Manalapan, a small town in Palm Beach County. It wasn't long before Lindsey agreed to his many requests to be his bride. While dining at the Top of the Tower, he got down on one knee and asked her to marry him, slipping a 2.5-carat 18K white gold diamond pavé engagement ring on her finger.

The dual going-away party and engagement celebration inside the four-office law firm included loud music, ring pops for some sweet bling, and several bottles of Rosé. Stacked trays of muffulettas from LaSpada's Subs and tea party sandwiches filled with cucumbers and caviar. Lance was clever—when Lindsey walked into the office that morning, he surprised her by filling her office with glittery banners, 24 vases of a dozen red roses, and a giant "congratulations" confetti balloon tied to her chair. The girls took turns smacking a piñata until the prizes broke free. Little candy dicks and packaged condoms fell out.

Donna brought in a homemade dick-mold vanilla cake, with pineapple rum cream syrup filling the top of the pecker.

Later that afternoon, Victoria and Donna helped pack Lindsey's gifts into her car. The girls working in the office gave her lingerie, sex toys, and cleaning supplies.

"I cannot believe my cheap-ass future in-laws gave me $500, and I've worked here for three years," Lindsey said politely.

"Shit, at least the old geezer wrote you a nice recommendation letter," said Donna as she grabbed her purse, pulling out a remote car key for her red Ford Mustang GT. "Where are you going so fast?" asked Victoria.

"Have to run home and give Sparkles his insulin shot before I meet you guys for dinner," said Donna. "I have to go home too. No time for dinner," said Victoria.

"Vic, please do not ruin my day by flaking out on us again, or I am sending little Danny to your house to kick that skinny Italian ass. We will have some girlie gossip aperitivo time like when we were all in Rome," said Donna.

"Oh, how I remember the quintessential cultural expressions of Italy at the end of the workday. Sorry, I must get home and prepare luggage for this weekend's trip to the Keys," said Victoria.

"Life is a big, tasty smorgasbord, and there are a lot of beautiful manly man sandwiches to try. Why miss out on a room packed with men getting off their boats?" said Lindsey.

"Yes, all right then, pain in my ass. Let us do this; it's your day, Ms. Vaughn," said Victoria.

"Trust me, it will be worth it, and I think you'll meet your soulmate tonight," said Lindsey.

"Yes, and then all of my dreams will come true. I, too, can quit this job, move far away from some real and some fake friends, and ride off into the sunset with tall, dark, and handsome to make babies," joked Victoria, as she thought maybe tonight could be the night.

The three girls shared many memories in that law office. Victoria held the door open as Lindsey pushed the balloons out, turning around to lock the office door. Wiping her eyes, she looked back one last time.

"Are you sad to leave us and this job?" asked Victoria.

"No, you weirdo. I was making sure the door was closed," said Lindsey, who often tried to be the non-emotional one in the group. Trying to sound cool and cheer her friend up, Victoria pulled down the passenger's sun visor while checking her hair in the cosmetic mirror. "Hey, Lindsey, would you happen to have any weed left from yesterday's burning session?" asked Victoria.

"Whatchu talking about? Now you are speaking my language. I will be rescinding my earlier character assassination of Ms. Victoria, as you are not a weirdo or even an airhead. You are rad, and you are my bestie now," said Lindsey.

Pulling out a green and yellow-flowered marijuana cross-body stash bag from inside the center console armrest box, they talked about how her life in Albany would turn out.

"Lindsey, would you slow the fuck down, girl? I know you are a happy adorable little stoner but let us make it to Happy Hour in one piece, Mrs. New York," said Victoria. "Didn't you see this huge rock on my finger? I am an insider now, Vic," said Lindsey as she held up her ring in front of Victoria's smiling face.

Marrying the well-connected Vaughn's hot son, Lance, means she is above the law. Between her parents and his, they make a completely untouchable pair. "Besides, whom the fuck would arrest this cheerful face?" said Lindsey.

The last thing we need is to get busted for smoking a doobie, thought Victoria. She gave a thumbs-up as they passed by two police cars parked on the side of the intersection of Goolsby Boulevard and Lock Road.

Before Lance, Lindsey had dated a pilot named Keith, a textbook narcoleptic. No one had ever diagnosed him until Lindsey discovered it. Keith graduated from aeronautical school with honors. The Strauss family snatched him right out of graduation with a six-figure salary. They were a wealthy coal-mining family with homes in Fort Lauderdale, Florida, and Jackson Hole, Wyoming.

She wrote in her diary about her boyfriend's condition, expressing that she had the best sex with him, simultaneously reaching climax until he would pass out. One summer day, they went on his yellow Piper, a small two-seater plane parked inside a hangar at the Executive Ivory Airport in Fort Lauderdale. He started falling asleep, and the plane began descending faster than usual. She punched his chest, freaking out, and he woke up. He called his doctor the very next day and was diagnosed with bipolar disorder and narcolepsy.

After seeing a fortune-teller who mentioned that the man she was with would die at a young age, Lindsey dumped him. Hearing this scared the heck out of her. Lindsey was just a young woman full of life, not deserving of an empty, lonely future. The young woman thought to herself, *who would raise my future kids when I'm a widow?* They remained terrific friends, but now that Lindsey was engaged, she told Keith to stop calling her, out of respect for Lance.

The restaurant's happy hour crowd usually consisted of small groups of parties that continued outdoors to the tiki bar overlooking the marina dock, where a Jamaican band played steel drums until closing. The high school friends started making eye contact with the same number of guys. The hottest of all bumped into Victoria and smiled with those baby blues. Looking at Donna from head to toe, he noticed the black museum dial with a silver-tone concave dot on her left wrist. One of the younger-looking guys looked at her and smiled.

"Is that a Movado watch?"

Victoria thought he liked Donna as he looked her up and down, smiling as if she were a piece of meat. "Yes, it is. We have matching watches," said Donna.

Victoria caught his eyes just as he looked at her, and she felt butterflies in her stomach once they made eye contact. He commented again about the girls' watch. "You have good taste. Yes, we have the same watch on. We'll get a table; sit with us.

We won't bite," said Blue Eyes. As Victoria sat down, she felt a bit of déjà vu. She felt embarrassed, thinking he might have thought she saw him as a sexist pig. Victoria sat next to Blue Eyes, who was at the head of the table. Across from her sat his brother, Angelo, with Lindsey to her left. Donna and the oldest brother, Salvatore, sat across from Victoria and Lindsey. The brothers had black hair and were all strikingly handsome at first sight. He was shy and appeared to be an observer, but after another cocktail or two, he opened up and whispered a few sexy remarks in Victoria's ear.

Victoria could hardly hear him between the loud music and the crowd. He pulled her chair closer to his to speak softly in her ear, placing his arm around the back of her chair.

They couldn't keep their hands or eyes off each other. "Victoria, you're rather quiet. I'm surprised that a beautiful girl like yourself doesn't have a ring on her finger. Boyfriend?" asked Angelo.

"No, well, yes," answered Victoria. She seemed confused by the question, and Lindsey kicked her under the table. "Is it yes or is it no?" asked Blue Eyes as he rubbed his hand down her back.

"Yes, I do have a boyfriend, well, no, not really. We broke up last week," said Victoria.

"What does he do?" asked Sal.

"He runs a construction company, which is his family's business," said Victoria. "What's his name? We may know him because we're in the same industry," said Sal. "His name is Antonio," said Victoria. She looked at Lindsey, hoping not to be kicked again.

"DiAngelo's Construction, his father owns it, and he runs it with his siblings. It's just off Summers Road," said Lindsey. Tony was nodding his head. The brothers couldn't believe it, all looking baffled at how coincidental this was. Tony, looking faint, placed his right hand on his head, wiping off his sweat. There was dead silence, as if there were an elephant in the room. Not confessing just yet, they thought this was crazy. What a small world.

"Why are you and this Antonio dude breaking up?" asked Blue Eyes, Tony.

"He's a great guy, a good family, but I'm just not ready to settle down and have children, and unfortunately, my father doesn't like him," said Victoria.

When the waiter asked Victoria for her order, Tony answered, "We'll both be having the salmon fillet with veggies, and please hold the garlic cilantro sauce." That was what she was going to say.

Tony kept pulling her chair closer to his and speaking softly to her about how happy he was that they had met. Victoria, now sitting even closer to him, could smell his cologne. "Okay, guys, guys, come on now, Tony. So, who wants to tell her?" said Sal. "Tell me what?" asked Victoria.

"Antonio, we call him Big Tony. The DiAngelo's are our family.

Our mom's brother is Antonio's father," said Angelo.

"Small world, and what a nice family you all have," said Victoria. She was shocked and nervous that she might have spoken out of line.

Donna and Lindsey were laughing. "We are cousins," said Sal. "I get that. Yes, I understand family lineage. Thanks, Salvatore," said Victoria sarcastically.

She felt a little silly now, having given away too much information. It was the last call; they were the only table left, and the girls had an early day at the law firm. Lindsey whispered into Victoria's ear, "Let him take you home. He's your soulmate," said Lindsey.

"It's bizarre; I can't believe they are cousins. I've never heard of them before," said Victoria.

The guys split the check three ways, leaving the waiter double the amount of the bill. They started walking out into the moonlight, seeing only three cars. Victoria laughed and sarcastically said, "Which ones are yours?" Three 911 Carreras were lined up at the valet; each brother had the same car, just a different color—red, black, and white. Tony asked Victoria to guess.

"I put my money on the black one," said Victoria.

They made out in the car and were the last to leave the parking lot. Tony drove Victoria home that night. She felt as if she had known him for a long time. They pulled up to her house, and the front entrance lights were brighter than usual. Her father must have been awaiting her arrival. She thought it would have been a lot cooler pulling up to the resort. "Since I drove you home, can I get your number?" asked Tony.

Without hesitation, she wrote it on the back of his business card. "It was nice meeting you, Tony," expressed Victoria. Laughing out loud at the young girl's innocence, he smiled at her, touching her face.

He smiled, wishing he had more time to spend with her. "It's Antonio, and it was very nice meeting you. Now get some sleep, beautiful girl," said Antonio.

Several weeks had passed, and she had never heard from him. This time, Victoria broke up with her boyfriend, Antonio, for good—or so she thought. A few days before Christmas Eve, someone banged on her front door. The housekeeper opened the door and found a wicker dog basket filled with toys and a folded-up note. Victoria opened the letter.

"I love you, Vic, and I am sorry. Please come over for Christmas dinner." The message read, "Vic, I will love you for eternity; you are my world. Love you so much, Babe, Antonio XO."

After a few unanswered calls, she finally returned his call. Antonio convinced her to stop the drama and come over. His mom had already invited Victoria's parents.

Carlos declined the invitation as he was in Hong Kong, having Christmas dinner with the Zhangs. His secretary sent a bottle of Opus One to the DiAngelos. Antonio had got his way once again.

Now, Christmas Day, and it could not have been a more perfect day—84 degrees, a heat index of 88, and humidity of 63%. The news called it a mostly sunny afternoon, with a chance of thunderstorms in the evening. Victoria drove over to the DiAngelo estate. They had a four-acre, four-thousand-square-foot estate home in Coral Springs. The Mediterranean-style home was built in 1970 by architect Gustavo Sapori, who had been designing homes for nearly forty years. The beautiful garden outside included Italian statues and a waterfall.

Victoria's mother, Sonia, arrived before Victoria and sat at the back table, speaking in Italian with Antonio's mother, Carmella, and Aunt Paulette, the cousins' mother. As Victoria entered the room, she thought, *oh no, what if Tony — Antonio, whatever his name is — is also here?* She figured she was safe, having a drama-free day. Carmella stood up to greet Victoria.

"How are you? Buon Natale," said Carmella. "Ciao bella. Come stai? Dove Pepe?" asked Victoria. "Pepe is with the boys, watching football," said Carmella. Victoria felt nervous, as she had never told Antonio that she met his cousins. She never had the opportunity because they had not officially broken up. It was just ignoring each other until one of them caved in.

Victoria hugged her mother. "Hello, I still don't understand why you had to drive without me," said Victoria. Walking to the bar, she approached Antonio's best friend, who was making a cappuccino.

"Hey, Vic, Buon Natale," said Christopher, kissing her cheek to cheek, thinking she looked hot.

"Merry Christmas," said Victoria.

"Has Santa been good to you? I don't think you've been a good girl, Vicky," said Christopher, winking at her. "I'm the perfect angel. You know Santa is always good to me," said Victoria.

As Victoria turned to leave, she caught him checking her out. Chris winked at her. He thought she could have been his girl, but he lost his opportunity, as he was loyal to his best friend, Antonio.

"You know what, Christopher, you are pretty funny," said Victoria as she winked back. She couldn't help but wonder if everyone already knew her secret.

"See how much froth is here. Now, this is how you make a cappuccino like a true barista. Where are you going so fast?" asked Christopher. "I am going to find Antonio," said Victoria. "Ciao bella," said Christopher.

Now, she was even more nervous. She fussed with her hair in the mirror, the familiar scent of cologne—black currant and apples—lingering in the air. A twitch in her knees hit her as she entered the living room. All three cousins were sitting on the couch next to Pepe, while Antonio sat in the recliner.

"Hey, babe, where have you been? You're so late," Antonio said. "You are worse than my brother Francesco."

Victoria leaned down to place the gifts under the tree. He reached for her, landing a big kiss on her plump lips and pulling her closer, squeezing her tightly. She could feel his cousin Tony's eyes piercing through her with disgust.

"Vic, meet my cousins Angelo, Salvatore, and Tony," said Antonio. Pepe had already met Victoria at the last family party. Pepe stood and hugged her hello. She looked over at the brothers, who barely acknowledged that she had even entered the room.

"It's a nail-biter—AC Milan just scored," said Sal.

Victoria felt strange; they were clearly ignoring her, so she excused herself to use the bathroom. When she walked out, Tony was standing there.

Victoria felt strange; they were clearly ignoring her, so she excused herself to use the bathroom. When she walked out, Tony was standing there.

"Hi, how are you? I wanted to call you, but I didn't know if you wanted to hear from me or not," said Tony.

"What is that cologne you're wearing? It smells so damn good," said Victoria.

"Why are you deflecting? I'm going to call you, that's it. I can't play this game anymore. We all thought you broke up with him," said Tony, leaning closer to her. She could feel he was wearing tight, well-fitted jeans.

Bianca, Antonio's youngest sister, walked out into the hallway. She was fifteen years old and could tell something was up.

"Hi, Victoria, I didn't think you were coming over today. Are you and my brother happy again?" asked Bianca.

"We have some things to work out. I have a present under the tree for you. I hope you like it. If not, you can exchange it," said Victoria.

"Grazie, Bella," said Bianca, running to the living room to fetch her present.

As they turned down the hallway, Tony grabbing for her back, pinched her ass with one hand gripping her hair at the nape of her neck while he kissed and nibbled on her throat as he held her hand tightly. He pushed her up against the wall.

"Are you insane? Do you want to have us both killed? Please stop," said Victoria. Tony couldn't stop caressing her. She smelled like roses, just as he remembered. He grabbed her other hand as she freed herself, pulling away from him. Smiling softly at her, he whispered in her ear, "OK, then. Later, you and me. 9 PM."

The rest of the day felt unusually tense for Victoria. Angelo was deeply absorbed in a conversation with her mother about Carlos's recent daring shark dive in Europe, while Victoria tried to keep her mind off the awkwardness. At dinner, Tony deliberately chose the seat across from her, his presence hard to ignore.

As coffee, after-dinner drinks, and an assortment of desserts, including refreshing cantaloupe, were brought to the table, the conversation shifted to real estate—specifically the brothers' local developments and upcoming mergers.

"What are the handsome brothers working on now? Any new construction projects that Carlos needs to be worried about?" Sonia asked.

"I see your signage showcasing a new luxury skyscraper in front of the Emerald vacant lot," she added.

Angelo smiled. "Yes, that was all thanks to me."

"Another luxury residence is exactly what Palm Beach needs," Sal commented, his tone reflecting both confidence and ambition, as he showed the rendering on his cell phone.

"That's a stunning building. I wish I could have secured that contract," Antonio said. The cousins often felt as though they were in competition with each other.

"Sonia, when are we going to put our girl Victoria to work for the family?" Antonio asked. "I know she needs to decide what she wants to do before Carlos returns."

Tony occasionally nudged Victoria's foot under the table, brushing it against hers. She felt the soft fabric of his touch on her leg and tried to stay composed.

Victoria was thoroughly confused—while she felt a sense of safety with Antonio, she found herself attracted to his cousin, Tony. The brothers seemed to be amused in her discomfort, watching her squirm in silence, unaware that Sonia, her mother, was oblivious to the subtle exchange. At times, Victoria's cheeks would flush bright red from her own embarrassment. Antonio remained unaware of the flirtation unfolding before him, although Sonia could sense the laughter and curiosity in the room, wondering what had prompted it. Tony's handsomeness was undeniable, and Sonia couldn't help but think her daughter was likely enjoying the attention more than she let on.

"As the evening drew to a close, it was time for the group to bid their goodbyes. The brothers briefly debated who would take their mother home. Tony attempted, but was unsuccessful, in catching Victoria's eye. She remained distant, unwilling to further engage in their subtle game of attraction. While Tony could not deny his feelings, he found himself drawn to her innocence and beauty, despite being aware that he was overstepping boundaries.

Victoria, on the other hand, recognized that she would need to confide in Zenya to fully understand the complexity of the situation. Tony, meanwhile, sought to prove to her that she could rely on him, though the significant age gap between them left him feeling vulnerable."

"Victoria walked to the window, watching Tony open the shiny car door. He was helping his mother, Paulette, into the fancy sports car. As Tony closed the passenger door, he glanced up at the window, winking at Victoria and smiling at her with one thought: *I'm finally back in her good graces.* He held up seven fingers to confirm their secretive plan. Victoria waved goodbye, silently praying that the damage from her spiked heel wasn't too evident within the grain of the Porsche leather seat—marking the first night of their love affair.

As she turned away from the window, Sonia approached her.

"I see what is going on here. My flirty daughter is being seductive toward the wrong family member. It's only puppy love. Do not ruin a good thing with Antonio. I know you will grow to love him more deeply someday. Don't listen to your father's tales and slanderous comments about his family ties with the mafia. Carlos will never think anyone is good enough for you. I agree that boy is gorgeous with those blue eyes, but he is all wrong for you, darling," said Sonia.

"Mom, you have it all wrong. Mind your own business and enjoy the party," said Victoria. She glanced at the time on her watch. *9 p.m. couldn't come any faster,* she thought to herself."

CHAPTER 5

GARNET'S LETTER

The morning began like any other. Garnet's visit was brief and left many unanswered questions—questions the children were not allowed to explore. Zenya wrote down the morning's tsunami dream. The family was in Greece and had to get to higher ground. Water was rising, and no one knew what was happening or when it would stop. The family was frightened. They ran on foot to a small, island-type car, hoping to reach higher ground. Water was rising above the white-and-blue roofs. Dogs and cats filled the narrow, winding streets, searching for safety.

The driver turned left into Seven Isles, where roads connected to small bridges and guard gates lined the entrances to the estate homes. The panicked driver reached the end of the bridge and slammed on the car's brakes. She noticed the water rising and realized she had no choice but to either back up the vehicle or drive straight into the crashing waves. They turned back around, heading toward the house they had just left. As they ran into the two-level house, the water was knee-deep.

Death and destruction filled the streets. It was as if a tsunami had hit the island. The volcanic collapse in the Canary Islands could have caused this. It was all happening too fast. Wiping tears from her face, Zenya wondered, *Was it real or just a dream?* She paused for a moment in her writing, reflecting on the heart-racing dream. Could landslides cause a mega-tsunami? She pulled the pink blanket over her eyes to shield herself from the memory.

The letters *HARPO* appeared in bold on the side of a yellow mustard-colored cargo ship, now on its side. All kinds of animals washed up on the sand—the island surrounded by the Ionian Sea, Mediterranean Sea, and the Aegean Sea. Inflatable orange rafts with asylum seekers had overturned.

The family made it to the top of the mountain, where the helicopter had been waiting. Zenya and Cash held hands tightly as they sat on Aurora's lap in the back seat of the small white car. Zenya now clearly visualized Chia driving the vehicle. As the family entered the helicopter, the father turned to the pilot and said, "We sure are happy to see you." Flying over the island of Santorini, they saw the blue-domed roof of the church with the white holy cross sticking above the water. Debris crashed into the sides of the mountain.

The little girl, now wide awake, continued to close her eyes tightly as she pictured her dream. Zenya wrote for about five minutes in her blue journal before she heard Sundance's distracting barks from the hallway. About an hour later, Benji would be driving the Zhang children to school.

"Yuan was outside discussing the market with Benji, reminding him that Amida had to take his karate test today. 'Have a nice day, children,' said Yuan. The children hugged him goodbye."

Chia was just about to ask when she could drive to school when her father spoke. "Chia, listen carefully— not today, not tomorrow, and not the next day. Benji is not just driving you to school and back. He is much more than that. He is your protection. There are bad people out there, and you should show a sign of appreciation to him, to me, and to your siblings. It's not just about you and how you look to your classmates. Safety comes first," said Yuan.

The black Mercedes drove away, and Benji waved goodbye from his cracked-open window. Today, Amida rode in the front seat next to Benji. As they pulled out of the estate home, Amida turned his head to speak to Chia. "You are an unappreciative person. Yuan is right about you," said Amida."

"Why do you feel the need to chime in? Please be quiet, and he is Father Yuan, not Yuan. That is disrespectful. What he said was I should listen before I answer. That is not mean. Why do you act as if it was an insult?" asked Chia.

"You think you are smart, and you are not," said Amida. The twins, Zenya and Cash, often finishing each other's sentences, simultaneously knocked on both of their heads. "Here we go again," said Cash. They held each other's hands tightly, then reached their hands over their ears to tune out the siblings arguing.

Driving down Victoria Peak, Benji could see a road-closed sign ahead. Strange, as in all the years working for the family, this

street had never had city workers. Benji had local police sensors installed in the car, but the system didn't have any reports. Every vehicle in its path showed up on the radar with green dots. These two vehicles were not even on his radar. As he stopped to turn right, a Mayflower truck blocked the road. They heard a loud noise, and the streetlights went out. The road was darker than usual. Benji pushed the safety alert button under the steering wheel to signal the Hong Kong Intelligence Bureau. The streetlights appeared to be out.

"Who is moving in or out?" asked Amida as he looked in the side mirror and saw an unmarked black Lenco Bearcat G2 SWAT truck.

"Benji, what the fuck is going on?" asked Chia. The twins

hugged each other while holding hands. Four men jumped out of the Mayflower truck with machine guns firing at the car.

"Guys, make sure your seat belts are on, please," said Benji as he turned the wheel and crashed into the back of the moving truck. The impact of the crash caused the Mercedes to flip over.

The whole situation felt as if it were in slow motion. Benji's heightened awareness was the reason the family hired him. The airbags deployed, and smoke rose from the dashboard, quickly spreading throughout the vehicle. Amida thought the car was on fire and was unhappy because he had chosen to sit in the front seat. Think about it: car accidents happen fast. One moment you're cruising along, and the next second, you're seeing stars.

The kids' ears were ringing from the noise of the gunshots, and the fear of shock was inevitably setting in for the Zhang children. The men raced back to the moving truck and took off, leaving skid marks on the road. Benji could see the moving truck in the rearview mirror. Although it was backward, he was able to memorize the license tag number: INF808.

Two men approached the Mercedes. Benji could open his bulletproof car door. Leaning down, he fired at them, shooting one in the leg and the other in the chest. Both men were dressed in black SWAT gear, including bulletproof vests.

"Benji, Garnet Zhang sent us. Hold your fire, son. The codeword is #808. We are from Infinity," said the gray-bearded man, who was wearing a black baseball cap with what appeared to be a horizontal version of the number eight.

Confused, Benji knew his only mission was to safely protect the Zhang family at all times. Intel immediately alerted Yuan of the accident. Benji heard ambulance sirens approaching the mountain. Yuan grabbed his car key, running out the back kitchen door into his ten-car garage. He jumped into the first car, driving down the road in his 2.5-million-dollar orange Bugatti Veyron 16.4 Grand Sport Vitesse. It was a short distance—only 8 minutes from the estate home. The vehicle's top speed is 255 mph, and he made it in less than two minutes.

Yuan jumped out of the car, not knowing what had just happened. He saw the green and yellow moving truck taking off and noticed the plate, INF808. Two unmarked police cars pulled up as the truck fled the scene moments earlier.

"Get after that truck," yelled Benji.

Yuan walked over to the car, bending down and looking through the windshield glass. Seeing all his offspring alive made him cry. Circling the vehicle and assessing the damage, the children quietly sat in total shock. They had been trained not to move in the event of a crash. Benji was alert and told him exactly what had happened, continuously repeating that he wasn't quite sure what Infinity meant or why they would say Garnet sent them, but he knew it was a clue.

Benji had to hurry and get the children out of the car, but he couldn't risk their safety. The engine leaked coolant, the radiator had cracked, the airbag propellant had a burnt-chemical smell of fire, the gasoline leak was worsening, and he feared an explosion. It was apparent those men wanted the Zhang clan dead. Paramedics pulled up and waited for Yuan's direction.

"Please take out Zenya first," ordered Yuan.

The paramedic reached for Yuan's youngest daughter and whisked her away into the ambulance. Amida, still with his seatbelt on, unable to feel his right arm and suffering from a pounding headache, figured he might not be able to take his scheduled black belt test that evening. The paramedics waited to move him to the Stryker Power PRO XT ambulance Cot last for fear of the unknown.

Yuan walked over to the ambulance as two crime scene vans stayed with the family, while one police car, with two officers, sped off with sirens blaring after the truck. Prying neighbors flocked around, watching the untouchable family in disbelief.

"Daddy, what is wrong with Chia?" Zenya cried out. Yuan picked up his little girl. She wrapped her arms tightly around his neck. With comforting words, he said, "Jellybean, Chia is safe. You are also safe. You still have two arms, one elbow with a neon green Snoopy Band-Aid, and two little chicken legs. Look, not even a scratch on you." Yuan touched her elbows and knees. "My little jellybean, no boo-boos. What an experience today with your sister and brothers! You'll write about this someday," said Yuan.

Seeing her father laugh gave her a sense of security. As she looked around at her siblings and up the road at the people staring at them, she collected her thoughts, realizing how lucky they were. She knew she would write down this car accident in her yellow journal. Although this story wouldn't fit the satire narrative, it would reflect her love for her siblings.

"Please treat Chia first. I see blood on her hand," said Yuan.

Chia was carefully yanked out of the car next; she nearly fell over, dizzy. Her head looked like it hurt. Good thing there were people around to help her. The smell of fuel leaking from the car didn't help much. Cash had to cover his nose to breathe properly. That's when he saw Chia's arms in a strange position.

A female paramedic with red curly hair and blue, fake-polished nails noticed the teenager's bent arms, confused by how they got that way—it didn't look right. She had a piece of glass stuck in her right hand and was leaning over as if she was about to faint. The pain must have been too much for her to bear.

Chia had been holding that glass mirror and putting on makeup when they crashed into the moving truck. A piece of the glass went into the side of her neck. She could see blood in her hand, but she didn't know where it was coming from, as she was in shock. Her hair was covering the piece of glass, and blood was dripping down inside her shirt.

Before Chia could even step into the ambulance, she collapsed to the ground and had a seizure. A cracked glass compact Chanel mirror fell beside her. Yuan rushed to his daughter, thinking the blood was from a bullet wound. Benji lifted the teenager into the paramedic's van. A small piece of glass was sticking out of the left side of her neck. As the car started to flip, Benji yelled to the kids to wrap their hands around their shoulders and brace for impact. Innocently, this must have been when Chia jammed the compact into her neck.

The paramedics observed that Amida exhibited signs of trauma. They extricated him from the front vehicle window and carefully positioned him onto a motorized stretcher equipped with a hydraulic lift system, allowing for both elevation and lowering at the push of a button. The paramedics then transported the four children to the nearest medical facility, with Yuan's consent.

While in the ambulance, they microchipped each of the children within seconds. Each child was discreetly chipped with the nano device. Infinity accomplished. Within minutes, they arrived at the hospital and were seen by the private Zhang family physician, Dr. Yates.

"Yuan, may I have a word with you?" Dr. Yates asked.

Yuan, standing outside the secret room, was baffled that his mother, Garnet, would risk his children's safety.

"Yuan, Garnet planned it the day prior, but she didn't want to be here in Hong Kong with your father, Xian, when it happened. Please understand that this appeared to be a random kidnapping and nothing more. The news media is already all over this. We purposely went under the radar today to have your children microchipped. The family was placed in a private hospital room, away from the reporters. The kids are here for CT scans and will soon be released. Headlines will capture a photo of the Zhang family unharmed," said Dr. Yates.

"Phil, I understand what you're telling me, but how could my mother hire a hitman? Those men could have killed all my children, for God's sake. Benji fired at those men. That was a murder attempt, and I want revenge. I need to speak with Garnet right now. Where can I find a secure landline in this hospital? I need to speak privately to her," Yuan asked. It was clear he was struggling to face reality.

"Garnet figured you would react this way. Here's what she gave me for you," said Dr. Yates. He handed Yuan an envelope with the Zhang logo on the top left corner. As he walked away, Dr. Yates turned back and looked at Yuan. "And by the way, those men had brass dummy bullets to give a realistic appearance," he added.

After flipping over the envelope, Yuan noticed the authentic, red-stamped Infinity symbol on the back. He pulled out two blank pages and realized he needed to use the UV light on his keychain. The handwritten letter, on luxury embossed paper, read:

Dear Yuan,

If you're reading this, it means the director of infectious disease has made a dangerous move—she has stolen the antidote. Her aim? To sell it on the black market. It's more complicated than that, though. She's convinced they're microchipping families with a cure for future immunity. The vaccine targets the DNA sleep cells and mitochondria, breaking down the body from within. The flu, autoimmune diseases, nothing will ever leave them. Someone must have leaked the secrets of Infinity.

The thing is the body can't shake it. When we sleep, we unknowingly repair our cells, lowering the risk of a lifelong viral infection. But not now. Do you see the connection? China was the first to harvest organs from the deceased long before the vaccine came into play. Those organs weren't just for flu vaccines—they were used to create the clones.

By now, my grandchildren have been microchipped—hidden beneath the skin of their right wrists. *You have to understand.* This was the only way to enroll them in Infinity without them ever knowing. Kidnapping, homicide, scuba diving accidents, suicide, or any bizarre "act of God"—all of it covered by the chip. It activates them into the superior 1% class, silently, without their knowledge. The plan was always this.

They could be anywhere in the world—lost, lifeless, their bodies unrecognizable. But the chip... *the chip would know.* It would detect the loss of their heartbeat, alerting the Infinity group. Within moments, a team of physicians would arrive, and they would be flown out—brought to the place we've always called "the end."

They will never die.

It's almost like that old fall alert system the elderly used to wear, but with much more at stake.

I can't ask you not to be angry. But I beg you—burn this letter. Then, take the children to the underground bunker with Benji. Do not contact Aurora. We must verify their organs are functioning properly—away from prying eyes. Trust no one.

Affectionately,
Xian and Garnet

Since birth, Yuan had the microchip and never really thought about its meaning. Garnet insisted on it because he was their firstborn and only son. Garnet never included Aurora in her Infinity will and last testament. Aurora was not of the Zhang bloodline, only by marriage, and Yuan never pressed the issue of his wife having the microchip. Besides, she didn't believe in any of the conspiracies. Half the time, Aurora was in her medicated world. She pretended to be an affectionate mother only when she wanted something. After the last pool incident, Yuan decided not to mention her poor parenting style to Garnet when caught in the act. The Zhang family would be calling a meeting for a trustee review with the family lawyer.

Approximately two hours had passed since the accident. The family's helicopter awaited the Zhang clan on the rooftop. Yuan found Benji in the hospital's private lounge, sipping a cup of coffee, and briefed him on their next course of action. They needed to reach the bunker before the reporters arrived.

Yuan struck a match and set fire to the letter, watching as ashes and smoke filled the air.

"Daddy, what was that?" Zenya asked.

"Nothing you need to know," Yuan replied. One by one, they filed into the helicopter. Aurora's calls flooded Yuan's cell phone, but he chose not to answer. His primary concern was the safety and legacy of his children. He placed a hand on Benji's back, once again thanking him for his unwavering loyalty to the Zhang family.

CHAPTER 6

KARMA

A few days before Memorial Day, Victoria was upset by her forgetfulness, bewildered and unsure of what to do or say. In her hurry to get to work, she had accidentally left her cell phone in Antonio's office after making a kind gesture of dropping off breakfast for him earlier that morning. Victoria had delayed working solely for Carlos, as she wanted to spend her first summer out of school with her friends. The lawyers had given the paralegals and administrative staff $100 gift cards to Wholesome Organic Foods.

Later that day, unbeknownst to her, Tony decided to get in contact with her finally. He couldn't stop thinking about her. He texted her one word: "Hello."

Antonio immediately called Tony. "Why are you texting my girlfriend, bro?" He felt like he was seeing red—cousins at heart, enemies at war.

"Bro, calm down. It's not like that. She just wanted me to get her one of those terracotta planter pots for her basil," Tony explained.

"When did you speak to my girlfriend to know that?" Antonio asked.

"Her friend is dating one of my friends. I saw her out a few weeks ago," Tony replied.

Antonio wondered if this was the whole story. What could be missing here? As truths are often diverse perspectives, the more viewpoints—and versions of events—one gathers, the closer they come to an overarching truth. The question now was: Did Antonio want to know the whole truth?

Antonio, a huge fan of Bruce Lee, was a member of the National Rifle Association. His peers call him a Bull's eye shooter, a skilled gunman who never left home without his Glock 17. His father Giovanni keeps a large selection of precision rifles, shotguns, handguns, surplus rifles and accessories, and sporting rifles and rifles in a locked room. "Fuck you. I don't believe the shit you say, and stay away from Victoria, or else I will break your face. She's mine. Or continue with the shenanigans and always look over your shoulder dickhead. You are a drug dealer, and we all know it." Said Antonio as he slammed the phone down. He could feel his pressure going up.

Later that day, when Victoria realized she had forgotten her cell phone at Antonio's office, she wondered if today might be the day Tony would unexpectedly reach out to her. With Lindsey gone and the office workload increasing, she was unable to leave early. The attorneys were fully immersed in a high-profile domestic abuse case involving a famous French novelist who had tragically passed away at 47 in Palm Beach. The office was abuzz with theories, convinced that the wife had hired a hitman after discovering her husband's affair with his 23-year-old Russian masseuse. Known for her flawless physique and as a well-known adult film star, she frequently traveled with her famous clientele, adding a layer of intrigue to the case.

After work, Victoria rushed to Antonio's office to retrieve her phone. She let out a sigh of relief when she saw that it hadn't been moved, naively thinking he wouldn't go through it.

Antonio looked tired, dark bags under his tanned skin. He was leaning back in an oversized black leather chair, his dirty black sneakers resting on the corner of the messy desk. With his right elbow on the desk, his hand pressed to his chin, he looked at Victoria with disdain. The metal cabinet, paper-filled office had several scratches and dents on the tabletops. His Glock sat securely in a holster on the side of his right belt.

He confronted her, asking how and when she had met his cousin. It felt like twenty questions. Victoria played dumb, insisting it was innocent. She repeatedly told him that nothing had happened and that he was being insecure for no reason. She left abruptly, saying she was off to meet the girls for happy hour.

Victoria never saw the text from Tony because Antonio had deleted it. He then left the phone in the same spot, watching her pick it up on the cameras. She met the intern Mike, Donna, and paralegal Rachael for their usual Wednesday night happy hour at the Cove. It wasn't the same without Lindsey.

Victoria's phone rang. It was Antonio, insisting she come over for dinner. He told her to hold on for a moment while he dipped a piece of ciabatta bread into the pot of his mom's homemade Bolognese sauce.

Victoria drove over from happy hour to see Antonio, never expecting to spend the night. When she reached for some water from the nightstand, she noticed a red rose in a glass of water behind the bed. His mother was into fortune-tellers and had tried to have Victoria's palm read, but that didn't go over so well with her. She was scared the "witch" would see right through her—confused, maybe even in love with Cousin Tony. How could she be? She had never believed in the idea of love at first sight. Yet, after months, she still felt this long-lasting attraction to a total stranger.

A week later, Donna saw Antonio at the farmer's market. They lived in the same neighborhood, and deep down, she never liked Victoria for being mean to her little brother. She also felt as if Victoria had come between her friendship with Lindsey. Donna spilled the beans, confessing to Antonio about that Wednesday evening at the Grove. The girls had met his three cousins during happy hour, followed by a two-and-a-half-hour dinner, which ended with Tony driving Victoria home. Antonio saw red.

"When you dump her, give me a call," Donna said.

It became a predicament for Victoria, as she had stronger feelings for the cousin. Regardless of whether they would be together, she didn't want to lead Antonio on any longer. He was a good guy and deserved to be happy, and in her heart, she wasn't ready to settle down and have a family.

Antonio and Donna started dating one week after that incident. Later that evening, Victoria called Zenya to fill her in. The time difference meant nothing; she needed to hear her best friend's voice.

"My love, walk away from anything toxic in your life. Whether it's a friend, family, or soulmate, we know anyone can emotionally release anyone. Concentrate on victory. Something fabulous always comes from something negative. Manifest a new soulmate in your life. Recognize that you deserve much better than what you've been with in the past. Time to release the past with forgiveness," Zenya said.

"I agree that the universe gives us what we ask for," Victoria responded.

"You don't need frivolous connections with people. You are independent, single, and beautiful. You're helping to run Carlos Holdings like a champ, and it's time you release these clowns from your life. Both Antonios are great, but without communication, you have nothing. You must make a choice or be single again," Zenya continued.

"I love and miss you so much, girl. You sound like Garnet when you preach to me. Sonia knew something was wrong during Christmas. I knew it was disastrous from the beginning," Victoria said.

About one minute after they hung up, Donna called Victoria. Lindsey was going to tell her if she didn't.

"Hi, Vic, it's me, Donna. Please don't be mad at me, but I saw Antonio," Donna said.

"How could you have forgotten to mention this to me?" Victoria asked.

"I just never thought about it. Again, I'm sorry," Donna said.

Victoria realized at that moment that Donna never truly cared about their friendship. With Lindsey in New York now, Donna no longer had any allegiance to Victoria. Her true colors were coming out. Victoria called in sick to the law firm the next day and flew to Hong Kong to spend the weekend with her father and hang out with her best friend, Zenya. While away, Tony called her and texted her, but she wouldn't answer because she didn't know what to say. DiAngelos had always been good to her, but ending it was the right decision. She was only in Hong Kong for the weekend and already felt like she had a clear head. She was finally able to think clearly. It was great to see her father and spend time with Zenya.

She flew back home on her family's private jet, and to her surprise, Tony was waiting for her on the side of the fenced-off tarmac at KPBI, Signature FBO.

"How did you get here?" asked Victoria.

Tony pointed to his Porsche and said, "I drove my car. How do you think I got here, Victoria?"

He was surprised she wasn't happier to see him—no display of affection, not even a kiss on the cheek.

"No, I mean, how did you know I was here right now, landing in Palm Beach?" said Victoria.

"Believe it or not, Sonia," said Tony.

"You called my mother?" said Victoria.

"Well, she technically told Sal, who then told me. He saw her at the tennis club," said Tony.

Victoria's driver was removing her Louis Vuitton duffle bag from the G5. Tony walked over to him, handed him $100, and said, "I will take Victoria home."

On the drive to Victoria's house, Tony asked her why she hadn't responded to his text a few months ago.

"What text message?" said Victoria.

"I knew it; he deleted it before you saw it. Did you ever leave your phone with Antonio, or maybe he had access to it without you knowing?" said Tony.

"Yes, I left it around Memorial Day on his desk," said Victoria.

Victoria told Tony everything she had learned about Donna seeing Antonio at the farmer's market. Tony realized she was innocent in all of this, and he didn't want to cause her any more embarrassment. Tony didn't care and never wanted to speak about his cousin again. They were family, but not close. He and his brothers only saw that side of the family on Christmas or at a funeral.

They went straight to her house from the airport, and he walked in with a bottle of champagne. She fell asleep in his arms. They dated for about three months, seeing each other almost every night. Tony would call Victoria on a whim, often visiting her at the law firm. Many evenings, he stopped by her place after work. He felt as if she was slipping away. Maybe he was already bored with her. The chase was over. It was a rainy Wednesday morning. He didn't know if he liked her for who she was, or only because it would piss his cousin off.

As planned, he picked her up at noon from her office. Always punctual, that was the one thing she liked about him.

"Where would you like to have lunch today?" said Tony.

"Let's do sushi," replied Victoria.

After a quick bite, he brought her to the beach and found an empty parking garage on the top floor, a perfect secluded area to have his way with her. The yacht, the airport parking lot, the hotel roof, Redwood Forest Park bench, the elevator at Breakers resort where he kept telling her to constantly move a little closer as he would kiss her neck and penetrate her as if it was a sign of affection. A bit naughty and creepy at the same time. Men needed a fancy-ass sports car to overcompensate for cocky attitudes, is what the girls back in Hong Kong would say. Dropping her back off at her office, he handed her a $100 bill and said, "Order from Gianni's. I will be over at 7 p.m. with the Chianti."

She felt naughty and relieved to have all her sexual pleasures filled by 1 p.m. in the afternoon.

Victoria learned that Tony had to pay off an assassin. They never really discussed anything about Antonio or that side of the family again. One evening, he was carrying a large amount of cash in a briefcase when he stopped by Victoria's house.

"What's in the briefcase?" asked Victoria.

"You do not want to know. Better off, you don't know what is in here for your own sake," said Tony.

"When are you going to work full-time at your father's office?" asked Tony, trying to change the subject.

Another month went by with meaningless sex, as it felt as if it wasn't ever going anywhere. Victoria knew she needed to break up with Tony—it was the best thing she could do for herself. Eventually, she grew tired of the storyline. This vendetta was just too overwhelmingly scary. She was in constant fear and never trusted Tony's motives. Did he like her, or was he trying to get back at his cousin for ratting him out about selling drugs years ago? This drama could ruin his reputation. Victoria did not have a clear conscience and knew nothing good would come out of this fairy tale.

Chapter 7

Old Friend's

Old boyfriends? Antonio? Tony who? It had been a solid two years, and they hadn't exchanged a single word. Victoria? She was on fire—single, thriving, and loving every minute of assisting her father, Carlos. Dating? Not even on her radar. She was a woman now, enjoying the thrill of a six-figure salary that still included spontaneous trips to dive with sharks on nearby islands with her dad. Then, Tony saw her face in a newspaper, and it hit him like a ton of bricks—he wasn't in love with her anymore, he was *in lust*. Victoria, a decade younger, fun, filthy rich, and drop-dead gorgeous, was like a dream he couldn't reach. She was the kind of wild beauty that fluttered just out of reach, an untouchable allure that he could only admire from afar.

The second leg: Hampton's getaway. Zenya flew to Miami for a friend's birthday party. It was the perfect weekend. While on the plane, Victoria discovered that Tony had been married the night they met. He had a son named Michael and was going through a divorce, and Victoria had no idea. The DiAngelo family knew very little about his personal life, other than that he was a successful businessman who shared a lucrative construction company with his brothers. They bought old buildings to demolish them and build condominiums along A1A.

Arriving at the Hamptons, best friend's Zenya and Victoria went straight to dinner. To Victoria's surprise, Antonio's brother, Francesco, was having a party at Vico's Italian Restaurant. Victoria was sitting at the bar with Zenya when she felt a tap on her shoulder. Turning around, she saw that it was Francesco. He had a goatee, a tan complexion, and looked fit, as if he had been working out. He now owned a large construction equipment manufacturer with headquarters in California and New Jersey. He was independent, self-confident, and determined to become the #1 equipment manufacturer in the world. He had a beautiful wife he met while on a business trip to Shutter Island. Her family owned a home on the island; the rest was history. Last year, they moved to Long Island and hadn't attended the infamous Christmas party.

"Victoria, you're looking good, babe," said Francesco. As they hugged, he explained that breaking it off was the best thing she had done because his brother Antonio wouldn't let it go.

"It's been a prolonged, bitter quarrel between my brother and Tony, and now his brothers are also involved," said Francesco. "Ladies, enjoy your dinner. Drinks are on me." As he walked away, he turned back, smiling at Victoria.

"He's handsome, Victoria. You went for the wrong family member," said Zenya.

"I know, and can you believe we share the same birthday and adore Yani? Francesco has always been trustworthy and has offered a sense of security and stability to everyone around him. He does take after his father," said Victoria.

When the girls asked for the tab, Vico replied that Francesco had already paid. The girls finished the bottle of Ruffino, giggling.

"I forgot—how did you meet Antonio?" asked Zenya.

"A group of us were at a Chris Johnson concert in Miami. Antonio had this nagging girlfriend by his side. I whispered in his ear as slipping my number on a folded-up cocktail napkin into his hand," said Victoria, laughing so loudly that tears were streaming down Zenya's face.

"You're kidding me. That's a funny love story. What did you whisper in his ear?" asked Zenya.

"To call me when he dumps her ass. He broke up with her that night and called Carlos the next morning to ask him for his permission to take me out on a date. It was not love at first sight. It was just me being aggressive and getting what I thought I wanted. Talk about the Law of Attraction. In hindsight, I should have just minded my own business," said Victoria.

"Hey, it's like when you drew a red heart around the senior quarterback's photo in the yearbook," said Zenya.

"Mauricio Capotti," said Zenya.

"Yes, good memory. Positive thinking—I manifested a boyfriend right my way. Damn, that ninth-grade yearbook. We should have burned it," said Victoria.

The girls were having a great time in the Hamptons and swore to return every year, no matter how busy their lives became. They spent a few days separately, visiting family and friends.

Victoria still couldn't get over the fact that she had dumped a great guy for his cousin. Her life could have been so different, she thought to herself. Her sister, Valentina, threw a party, which was perfect since Zenya was still in New York visiting her grandmother, Garnet, and they were both included in the festivities.

Lindsey, now calling Niagara Falls home, arrived at the party in style—by helicopter. A few hours before the festivities, she and her old friends squeezed in a game of tennis and a light bite, all while sipping on a crisp bottle of rosé. Victoria couldn't help but laugh as she recalled that wild story about Keith, the pilot. Back in the '90s, no one was talking about narcolepsy. But Lindsey? She still had Keith's case studies saved on a disc, a secret she'd never breathed a word of to anyone.

One day, there was a knock on her front door. Two CIA agents pushed down the door, pulled her against the wall, and patted her down. She was genuinely shocked, as she had never told anyone other than Donna and Victoria. She was surprised that her parents didn't know about this.

Lindsey was the prettiest girl in high school, with ivory skin and auburn curly hair. She was the girl Victoria smoked pot with for the first time. Having ties with the Presidential Campaign put her in a different category entirely. It was no wonder she could talk her way out of anything. Her father is still a lawyer, now living in New York to be closer to his daughter, and working for the District Attorney's office.

The CIA had the case study in their hands, and she sat down and told them everything. She found out that he was with his fiancée, flying over Peanut Island when the plane took a nosedive and plunged into the Atlantic Ocean. The fiancée died, and he claimed he tried to remove her seatbelt, but it wouldn't release. This was a proven lie, and he is now serving life in jail for narcolepsy. That could have been Lindsey. Her favorite phrase was that life is not a dress rehearsal. To this day, she says she lives life to the fullest every day and recently purchased a cottage home in Niagara Falls.

Lindsey is an LGBTQ wedding planner and the owner of Strawberry Bells & Floral Designs. When New York passed the law, she opened up a B&B for her guests. Her mom died last year from breast cancer, so she doesn't settle.

Lindsey didn't bring Lance. "I caught him fucking some girl he met at the gym, so I dumped him. Our marriage is over." It was her second dirty martini, and she was sharing the news that she had been dating NY's Anthony Gaddie, the NY mob crime boss, on and off. He was her sugar daddy. She was allowed to use his black card, and, boy, did it come in handy for her new B&B venture—until she discovered that the Feds had canceled her card. It was no coincidence that the same day, she saw on the news that the crime family empire was crumbling. He is now serving life in prison.

To no surprise, Donna, the bully from high school, married an FBI agent and now lives in Miami. Her father had been mayor of Palm Beach for more than seven years before becoming the governor of Florida. She still runs in the same circle of friends as Victoria. But after her little romance with Antonio she knew she would always be a backstabber. Another lady, whose husband is on the board of Ginsanto, a food chain that continues to gain criticism for being a known supplier of genetically modified foods, lives in Seattle and also has a home in Manalapan.

Shelly is another lady who lunches. She is married to oil tycoon Tehran Sohaed, who flies back and forth from Libya on their private plane. They rent a two-bedroom home on the beach while building a house on the water off Worth Avenue. Lindsey has always had groups of friends, but she sure gravitates toward the more affluent ones. The tale of two Antonios looks much better on paper, where it needs to stay for eternity.

Not going back at this point, she thought to herself. Victoria knew it would once again lead down a rabbit hole to nowhere land. She wondered, What kind of insecure girl would have admired a selfish person who never asked a question? Year after year, when they would rekindle their friendship, he thought it would be back to *Bada Bing, Bada Boom!* He was wrong, as Victoria wanted no part of that. She needed to get to know the person again, not live in the past. Who wants to reminisce when we're here now, in the flesh, older, with money and success? He had always been the adventurous type—very active and alert. It was often in the early morning hours when he'd find that he must succeed in planning his day, squeezing her in for a quickie at the port, on a park bench, in the elevator, or in the stairwell. Anything out of the ordinary was his speed. Or so she thought. Perhaps this was just an act to make it seem naughty, adhering to the playboy attitude and not bringing the girl home for Mama to meet.

That has always separated the marrying types from the single women of the world. Most girls with a crush drop lace panties too quickly. Girls need to educate men on how they want to be treated upfront, telling them, "These are the rules: three strikes, and you're out." Starting to talk to one another every few years is pointless without courting. Grandmother Garnet's point of view has always been that a man needs not just to woo a woman, but also to be genuinely nice. She would tell the young, naïve girls that the early bird may catch the worm, but the caterpillar turns into a beautiful butterfly.

One day, the caterpillar stops eating, hangs upside down from a twig, and spins a silky cocoon into a shiny chrysalis. This ugly caterpillar transforms its body within its protective casing, eventually becoming a beautiful butterfly or moth. It is no surprise that a moth would remember what it learned in the later stages of its life as a caterpillar. She will remember what was discovered later in her life, concealing the truth. Similarly, a woman must shed her thick skin to find the love of her life.

We believe in timing, yes, but as true soul mates, they would respect one another's feelings. Zenya tells the story of the fisherman who went out to sea one calm morning, only to drown in a storm. The mermaid must have captured him, as his wife stayed home that day. Men can always find hotter and younger girls out there, was the moral of the childhood story. Just when the caterpillar thought the world was over, it became a butterfly.

While walking alone on the beach in Montauk, Victoria couldn't stop thinking about Tony liking that hot young Mexican girl he met at the beach club. When he mentioned Mexican food, she knew that was code, and boy, is karma a bitch? She bites back. He will always be the same immature skirt chaser in her eyes, trading his girlfriends in for the younger, newer model. She knows in her heart that she deserves a man with substance. She is not a puppet on a string; he may think he is in control, but he does not know a thing. Victoria thought, *checkmate*. In this story, she is the one who checkmated a triumphant checkmate. Once announced, he soon realizes the loser in this chess game has been him all along.

Victoria and Zhang were *buzzing* with excitement as they headed to the hottest event in town—a dazzling white party at Infinity, just off Main Street, on the last night of the season! It was a celebration like no other: the 95th birthday bash of the legendary Mary Ann Song, Ph.D., CEO of Vellers, the groundbreaking company that revolutionized genome sequencing!

The party was electric—a whirlwind of laughter, music, and glittering lights. It ended with a spectacular fireworks display and champagne toasts to Mary Ann, a trailblazer whose work has shaped the future of pharmaceutical drug discovery and global manufacturing. Dr. Phil Yates took the stage, his voice filled with pride. "It is with great honor that I introduce Dr. Mary Song, the brilliant mind behind the groundbreaking science of COVID vaccine development!" The crowd erupted in applause! They danced all night under the full moon.

Chapter 8

Victorias' Visions

It was a Sunday afternoon, and the energy in the air was palpable as the Hamptons crowd flocked to roads, and helipads, eager to head back to the city. But something caught Victoria's eye—a black VW Jetta parked by the side of the road. It looked out of place, almost *too* neutral. No one claimed it, and just as she suspected, it started to roll, heading straight for the other parked cars.

Suddenly, with a screeching slide, the car careened off the road and splashed into the Great South Bay Intracoastal waters.

Victoria's heart raced as she watched families spilling out of Church-by-the-Sea, none of them aware of the looming danger. A knot twisted in her stomach, the kind that only comes when *something big* is about to go down. Sitting in a limo, her instincts screamed, and when she turned around, her eyes widened in shock—an *enormous* wave was speeding straight for them! Water surged up onto the road, and in a split second, Victoria's worst nightmare, her recurring tsunami dream—was coming to life.

"*Drive now!*" she screamed, panic creeping into her voice. The driver's eyes widened, but there was no escaping the enormous, roaring wave bearing down on them. The street turned dark and dreary as the sea grew closer, the sound of crashing water filling the air. It felt like *doomsday*—and the only escape Victoria could think of was to *fly*. The driver pushed the accelerator, but the giant wave was relentless, closing in fast.

Oddly, it was the beginning of summer, yet thick layers of snow and ice coated the roads, and the wind turbines had stopped working.

They reached the underground facility, and the scientists grabbed Victoria's hand, running as fast as they could into the concrete building. Residents heard the emergency air raid siren sounding in the far distance. Over the loudspeaker, first and last names were called out. Zenya looked at Victoria and asked, "Do you know what time it is?" as if she had a secret. Victoria glanced at the Cartier watch Carlos had gifted her for her 21st birthday. "It's 3:00 p.m.," she answered.

Zenya was baffled that they had been having the same recurring tsunami dreams since childhood. "You know what I'm thinking? We can get to the bottom of this. The Long Island

Railroad runs trains to the Hamptons. After reaching Westhampton, it's about two hours to Montauk. That train is about to pull in here any minute, and you know who will be on that train?" Zenya asked. Wiping her tears and now smiling from ear to ear, Victoria said, "The great Dr. Yates." The girls stopped talking for a moment, looking at each other. Then, pointing at the white plane, they saw a man getting off a Harley Davidson near the aircraft. "Here's our chance. Let's go see if he can fly that Hawker!" said Victoria.

The girls ran over to the plane. As they entered the aircraft, they noticed a coat closet on the left side, just off the main entrance door. The floor was stacked with snacks, champagne, and Fiji water bottle boxes. Directly across on the right-hand side was the main galley. The main cabin featured a four-place club, followed by another club seating arrangement with fold-out card tables. Further aft was a full-service lavatory with one left-hand belted toilet that was externally serviceable, followed by a heated and pressurized baggage compartment. Forward Cabin Pocket Doors. The cabin seats nine passengers. Victoria smiled at Zenya and the baffled-looking man. "We can fit comfortably on this plane."

"We will need your help. Can you fly it? We must get out of here; we have no time to waste," said Victoria.

The middle-aged man, wearing caterpillar steel-toe boots, blue jeans, and a Hells Angels leather vest over a white Hanes crewneck T-shirt, looked down at his inexpensive yet practical Casio G-Shock watch.

"Yes, ma'am, I'm your guy. I just need to fuel up and contact our cabin attendant," said Pilot Earl.

Zenya knew they were running out of time as she glanced toward the train station.

"No need for an attendant. Please, sir, we need to get out of here and head down to Montauk," said Victoria.

Hurrying onto the plane, they rushed to the train port, hoping to find him.

The underground high-end express train pulled into the port, and the girls anxiously awaited his arrival. As Dr. Yates exited the train, he saw their ghostly pale faces. Something seemed very wrong.

NASA Office of Inspector General (OIG) Samuel Madison stood waiting for Yates's arrival. Holding a cigar and wearing aviation sunglasses, he said, "Zenya Zhang, we finally meet. Are you here to redeem your Infinity Chip?"

"What chip?" Zenya replied, confused.

"Nick Dupre. Our paths keep crossing. I would think you've been stalking me," said Victoria.

"We are here to investigate the missing person incident from last weekend. We understand you were all attendees of the Infinity Fundraiser. Can you tell us anything out of the ordinary?" said Nick.

"It was a typical Hamptons party," said Zenya.

"Did anyone say anything, perhaps a code word, or hand anyone a business card? Maybe even a brochure about death?" asked General Madison.

"Someone mentioned a 3-0161 experiment. It sounded like a fantasy movie about the apocalypse," said Dr. Yates.

"I don't recall anything odd, other than the conversation about weather control. And today, we had an afternoon of 90-degree weather full of sunshine, which turned to darkness, snow, and ice—with a tsunami warning," said Victoria.

CHAPTER 9

PLUS, ONE

The weather forecast predicts an 81% chance of rain in the area, yet not a cloud is in the sky. Snow is melting on the steps of the four-bedroom brownstone. It was a record-setting month in May, and the news reported that 7.8 inches of snow fell in Albany. Zenya is spending more time with her older sister now that she is interning at the Carlos Holdings New York headquarters.

Chia's graduation party went into the wee hours of the night—a celebration at Lobar's with twenty-five of her closest friends, including a few Zhang family members. Laughter echoed around the room, coming from Zenya's long-time friend, seated at the Zhang table. The girls met when they were ten years old, the year Carlos moved the family to Hong Kong. His daughters enrolled in the same private school that the Zhang children attended. Some of them formed bonds that will never break, no matter what happens. Zenya and Victoria swear they are sisters. They are best friends, even though they have lived on different continents. They share everything. A friend can tell you things you don't want to say to yourself.

Victoria's father, Carlos, is Italian, and her mother is Spanish, which contributes to her speaking multiple languages. Her professional work attire typically includes St. John and Chanel suits, while at home she prefers Ralph Lauren resort-style clothing when she's not in her gym clothes. Victoria grew up living with her father's parents in the late '80s in Palm Beach, Florida. In 1991, when Victoria was ten years old, her grandfather relocated the family to Las Vegas, and they also had a third home in Hong Kong.

The first time Victoria can remember having a tsunami dream, she was eight years old. She was awakened in the middle of the night, screaming. Sonia, her mother, thought she might have been acting out for attention. Victoria was fascinated by Bruce Lee and earned her black belt at just 12 years old. Nearly a polyglot, she spoke Spanish, Italian, Cantonese, and English. As a child, she often daydreamed about becoming a famous scriptwriter. Classmates frequently nominated Victoria to play leading roles in school plays, including the tooth fairy, a teacher, an actress, and a fashion model. Her mother submitted several short stories Victoria had written as a kid. One of them was titled, "Mommy, why on earth is the sky red?"

"Why do you think it's red and not blue?" Sonia asked.

"Because God is BBQ'ing," replied Victoria.

Martin Chantal III was engaged to Victoria for about a day before the relationship ended badly, resulting in a restraining order. They had planned to marry in Ocho Rios, Jamaica, best known for its beautiful beaches and fishing village. She also attended Teen Boards of America. Her current "flavor of the month" is boyfriend Victor, a strikingly handsome man and a pilot. They've been dating for a year now, though, in the world of pilots, that's just three months since they're rarely around for long.

Victoria is a born-again Christian who turned to practicing Buddhism at a young age. She is an earthy Taurus who loves luxury. Intelligent, ambitious, and trustworthy, Taureans are often considered the anchor of the Zodiac. They have amazing friends, colleagues, and partners, and they value honesty.

Taureans are proud of their drama-free relationships and will walk away from anyone, even family, who does them wrong. They won't support nonsense, and as Bulls, they've earned a reputation for being stubborn.

This searching sign is willing to consider another point of view, but they will never flip-flop on an opinion just to make someone else happy. They are not people-pleasers and will only change their thinking if they genuinely have a change of heart.

A detail-oriented Taurus may seem nitpicky—even in the bedroom. A mid-romp critique might not be unusual, but it's not because they want to offend. Taurus will hold a grudge against someone who lies, even if the lie is told to make them feel happy. In bed, Taurus is a giving lover—as long as their partner steps it up and makes sure to give and receive pleasure. They demand the best, and they expect the people in their life to deliver. If not, they'll banish them to the bottom of their heart for eternity.

Chia graduated from FIT. She began a two-year associate degree (AAS) program directly after high school. Chia has always been a gifted student, quickly grasping new information. She never got along with Aurora, who never praised her children for any achievements, continuing to criticize Chia until it was decision time. Chia refused the offer to attend boarding school in Switzerland and instead pitched her parents on staying in the same city as Grandma Garnet, who is now 80 years old and all alone. The decision was whether to spend more time watching over her younger siblings, Zenya and Cash, or to move out of the estate home.

Chia completed her AAS and applied to a two-year bachelor's degree (BS/BFA) program majoring in Fashion Design. It was no surprise that Victoria never bonded with Zenya's immature sister, Chia, as she sometimes acted out on that demonic side of her Gemini traits. A Gemini, very much a double-sided girl. Despite Chia's sociability and inexhaustible energy, she was also insecure and vulnerable. Over the years, it had been easy to offend her. When Zenya and Victoria would go off to group events without inviting Chia, she would take it personally. Gemini signs don't tend to offer many compliments or pay much attention to others. They will pout nine out of ten times and won't talk to you for a long time. A Gemini is empowered to criticize people, but it's unacceptable to blame those born under this sign. It touches the strings of their soul that are too fragile.

Yuan refused to let Chia live on campus, hoping she would stay with his mother. Chia convinced her father to purchase a $4,000,000 townhouse, a beautiful brownstone off Park Avenue in Murray Hill's Historic District. Her long-time boyfriend, Yeung, moved to the city with her. His parents didn't mind.

Had he stayed in Hong Kong as a young boy, he would have continued living in his 30th-floor, 280-square-foot nano smart apartment with no ambition, working as a DJ at the ZK Nightclub.

Yuan used to say he was waiting for his inheritance money, but his aunts and uncles were all neighbors living in Hong Kong's 120-square-foot crammed coffin apartment homes in the Yau Tsim Mong District. Yeung started as a bellman and worked his way up to a hotel manager at the Pierre Joutte on Park Avenue. Abbey, Victoria's first cousin, called her this morning at 7 am.

"Hear me out before answering. Be my plus-one at a wedding in the Keys. It'll be low-key, just what you need," said Abbey.

"A wedding? You're out of your mind, Abbey?" replied Victoria. "I will also be fixing you up with someone."

"Listen to me. I'm not interested in being set up. No way, no how. I'm hanging up unless you have some other breaking news to share," said Victoria.

"You're no fun, and no, I didn't see anything earth-shattering on GNN this morning. It's not up for debate because you're coming as my plus-one. Conor McAdams RSVP'd, and we all know you're a perfect match. We described you as an all-American beauty, having the same look as Heather Locklear — just with a Latin-American twist. Don't you remember the tall kid from the Hamptons with red hair and freckles?"

"Wait, Yeung? Chia's boyfriend?" said Victoria.

"No, not him," said Abbey. "I repeat, not interested in being set up with this Conor guy, no way, no how," said Victoria.

A few weeks later, after breaking off her engagement and having her heart broken for the first time, she decided, "Why not?" with a little help from Abbey. The plan was for Victoria to meet her cousin at 4:50 pm at Fort Lauderdale Airport. Of course, she would have preferred to offer her family's plane, but Victoria didn't want to come across as controlling. Plus, she was now open to meeting someone new.

Valentina and her boyfriend Paul dropped her off at Fort Lauderdale Airport. They couldn't wait too long inside with Victoria, as they were already late for the Hangar party at the Resort. They were in town for the annual Boca Raton Resort Antique Car Show—tonight, Jay Yeno was speaking. Professional golfer Paul Sanes was a guest speaker. He had won the PGA Championship the year prior and was doing Jay a favor by attending.

"Where the hell is Cousin Abbey? What time is her flight arriving? I want to say a quick hello, but we can't wait much longer," said Valentina.

"Hey, Paul, is my sister always this uptight?" asked Victoria.

"Not really," said Paul.

"Calm down. God, why complain about shit you can't control? Abbey will be here any second. Just sit tight, and I'll get a few coffees and pastries," said Victoria.

"Thank you. I'm sorry, we have to get to Boca," said Valentina. Paul handed Victoria a $50 bill, and she nodded as if to say, "I've got it." As Victoria walked to the barista stand, she felt someone touch her right shoulder.

Abbey snuck up behind her, saying "BOO" as she tugged on the back of her shirt. They hugged each other, as if it had been a while since the cousins saw one another. Victoria's first impressions of her cousin's best friends were that they were your typical Jersey girls. Susie, a runway model, was dressed in tight Levi's and black thigh-high boots. Nadine was an aggressive, loudmouth Bostonian with an impressive way of debating. As they were all standing at the car rental counter, Nadine convinced the minimum wage employee to upgrade her vehicle to an intermediate one. In the end, she won the debate at no additional cost. Julie was an actress who played Meadow in the 90210 series.

The girls' four-hour midnight run to Key West was worth the trip. They told stories about boys, shared great laughs, and quickly got to know the infamous cousin, Victoria. Susie imagined traffic would be a nightmare because the initial stretch of road from the bottom of the Florida peninsula to Key Largo was mostly one lane in either direction.

"You know, there are a lot of great places to stop along the way to Key West," said Nadine.

As if reading a children's story, but actually reading from a Key West brochure, she continued, "What to Know About Key

West. When is the best time to visit Key West? Key West has temperate weather, with temperatures ranging from the 70s to the 80s year-round. The highest amount of rainfall, averaging around 5.4 inches, tends to occur in August and September.

"Are there fun events in Key West I should be attending?" asked Victoria.

"Many different festivals occur throughout the year. These include Pride Week, Lobster Fest, Hemingway Days, and more," replied Nadine.

"What recreational activities are there in Key West?" asked Victoria.

"Kayaking, dolphin encounters, diving, and snorkeling are popular excursions," said Nadine.

It was a riot, and the girls knew they would have a weekend filled with great memories. Nadine was starving, and stopping at the first McRonald's along the way wasn't Victoria's first choice, as she was a vegan.

"You don't want anything, Victoria?" asked Abbey.

"No thanks. Eating reconstituted, deep-fried meat and saturated fat isn't my thing," replied Victoria.

Her reply kicked off an exhausting half-hour Q&A session on why and when she first decided to become vegan. The girls asked if she was a member of PETA. After the Jersey girls devoured unhealthy deep-fried chicken McNuggets and French fries, everyone grew quieter. Victoria quietly ate an organic nutrition bar as she stretched out on the uneven and bumpy floor bed, compromising by using her black leather duffel bag as a pillow.

Later, upon waking, Julie said to Victoria, "Well, you sure know how to make yourself comfortable anywhere." Laughing out loud, Victoria knew how true that was.

Arriving at Key West at 4 am brought back memories for Victoria of her time with Martin. Passing resorts where they once had fun-filled days on wave runners and romantic dinners in the heart of the Florida Keys—nothing like it, straight out of a Hemingway novel.

Entering the timeshare condominium, Susie volunteered to sleep on the couch in the living room so that the cousins could stay in one bed, and Julie and Nadine could stay in another. They talked about watching the sunrise at 6 am before sleeping until 9 am. As the girls awoke after only five hours of sleep, they excitedly put on their swimsuits and made their way to the Wyndham Resort & Spa in laid-back old Florida Keys. They lounged poolside while overlooking the ocean, with waiters continuously catering to their every need with fruit-flavored ice pops, rum cocktails, and chilled forehead towels. Victoria walked over to the beach bar and purchased a fresh fruit cup and a long-time favorite old-fashioned Bloody Mary with a shot of vodka and extra horseradish.

Later in the day, after two Bloody Mary's and much good tanning time, the groom, Craig, arrived poolside with some of his single friends. Abbey decided to go on a wave runner with her stockbroker co-workers. Nadine, Victoria, and Julie agreed to stay poolside and soak up some more Key West rays.

Then Conor, Matt, and Craig approached the girls, and Nadine whispered that the tall one was Conor. Victoria didn't wait for an introduction; she stood up, put her right hand out, and said, "Hello, nice to meet you. I'm Abbey's cousin."

"I KNOW!" Conor replied quickly. "I think you know my brother John. I don't remember either of you—I was bounced around to a lot of schools growing up," said Victoria.

Victoria's first impression was that he was tall, about 6'2", and oddly quiet. She was surprised because she had heard that Conor was obnoxiously rude at times and the life of the party at others. Victoria was feeling no pain after Conor bought the second round of lemon drops. It was a good choice, Victoria thought to herself. Not being able to finish the shot, she dumped it into what remained of her Bloody Mary.

By 3 pm, the girls decided it was time to head back to the condo and get ready for Craig and Yolanda's wedding. Victoria had broken out in hives the day prior and went to see her Primary Care Physician, who told her not to worry about it as hives are a sign of stress.

Victoria had called off her wedding plans after the night of her infamous bachelorette party. She had to explain the drama to her family and friends without giving too much detail, which often leads to exaggerated stories behind her back. Only one month later, attending someone else's wedding might have been too much for Victoria.

The girls made it to the wedding just in time, taking their seats on the dock. Abbey sat next to Victoria, right behind them. Nadine, Julie, Matt, and Conor sat in the next row at the far end. Victoria was doing just fine until the end, when the groom kissed the bride, and she stared out into the ocean. The wedding gazebo was at the end of the pier, with the archway elegantly filled with white roses, peonies, and sage eucalyptus.

Victoria thought, *This was supposed to be me.* She had always wanted to get married on the beach. Close to losing it, she looked away, out at the beautiful Atlantic Ocean, with a tear in her eye. She repositioned her body to the right, where no one could see her emotions flying or another tear dripping from her ankle-length black dress.

As she turned, she caught Conor's eyes behind her, with a tear in his eyes simultaneously. Knowing his recent divorce status from her cousin's earlier briefing, she almost felt bad for him. She realized how silly she was for not going through it, as he did for three long years. How could she be upset when he was the one who had been married? Though it was years on and off with Martin Chantal III, she still, at that moment, felt the emptiness and the void she had tried so hard not to accept.

Vic's first tear dropped since that God-awful day she called it off and gave Martin the engagement ring back. The thought of her big day made her run inside Don Shula's bar, ordering a cosmopolitan. The rest was history—well, just for half a chapter.

CHAPTER 10

REBOUND

A year had passed in the blink of an eye, and time was flying by for Zenya and Victoria, who had both been working tirelessly. Despite their busy schedules, they managed to meet up several times throughout the year, and something incredible had happened: John and Conor McAdams had become regulars in their circle. The brothers were now inseparable from Cash and the girls, spending countless hours together. It was clear— there was no denying that the McAdams brothers had firmly woven themselves into this dynamic, vibrant group of friends, creating a bond that only grew stronger with time.

Abbey called Victoria to check on Uncle Carlos. "So, how's he doing? Is he still in the fight of his life?" Abbey asked, her voice laced with concern.

Victoria's response was dramatic, as always. "He's in the hospital—thank God he's okay. It all happened in Australia. The shark circled him again. His heart was pounding so hard it felt like it might explode, and every breath he took felt like he was drowning. And all he could think about was not being able to walk me down the aisle one day."

Abbey listened for a few minutes as Victoria filled her in on Uncle Carlos' latest battle with his health. But she couldn't hold it in any longer. "Okay, okay, enough of Uncle Carlos and his dramatic shark attack. I've got something I need to spill."

Victoria raised an eyebrow, even though Abbey couldn't see her. "What is it now? You're not going to tell me one of the McAdams brothers is going for round two of their theory on 'forever' wedding bliss, are you?"

Abbey chuckled. "Well, guess what? Conor's doing it. And this time? He's convinced it's 'the one.'"

Victoria went silent for a moment, letting the absurdity of it all sink in. "Wait. Who's the poor girl this time? Let me guess… some Sicilian princess who's going to trap him in another 'Romeo and Juliet' kind of mess?" she scoffed, her voice dripping with sarcasm. "Honestly, what's his deal with Italians? The man's Irish, for crying out loud. And thank God Zenya's thing with John also fizzled out. That was almost as ridiculous as the idea of me marrying Martin. I guess, at this point in our lives, it's tough to find the right one. I think you lucked out with Matt. As for Zenya and me, it's been tough dating, considering our families are constantly in the limelight of Page Six."

The cousins were still chuckling on the other end of the line, their laughter echoing in the air. Abbey finally broke the silence, "Does he dream about being a Godfather or what?"

Victoria rolled her eyes, but the smile was evident in her voice. "More like a consigliere. You should've heard him back in the day. Conor used to talk about remarrying, having kids, living some ideal life. Honestly, I used to laugh at his big plans and his over-the-top ways. But, you know, I kind of get it now. That day—sipping martinis outside the Palisades Hotel on Las Olas Boulevard—I just remember thinking how nice it would be to hang with him a little longer, just to enjoy that moment together. They came from money, sure, but what I didn't realize was how much we were intertwined, how close our lives actually were."

Abbey hummed in agreement. "You guys were practically neighbors back in the day, right? But you never met until I introduced you to Conor in the Keys. I still think you're both wrong and were just embarrassed that you had a crush on each other when you were younger. I also think you met him when you were staying in the Hamptons that long summer break—when Carlos let you stay alone in the house, knowing the Zhang clan was all at Garnet's place just up the street. And I bet Zenya really does like John. You two could be sisters-in-law. The world's a funny place like that."

"Yeah, it really is. His dad was a gambling buddy of Carlos's, but somehow, Conor and I never crossed paths as kids. It wasn't until you introduced us down in the Keys that we actually connected. I swear."

Abbey raised an eyebrow, her voice teasing. "And his family—the Sanderbilts? That always seemed to catch your attention better than his last name. But Victoria McAdams also has a nice ring to it."

Victoria laughed softly, a hint of nostalgia creeping in. "Oh, come on. I mean, who wouldn't be intrigued? His mom's side of the family is practically royalty. The Sanderbilts—Martha Hogwarts lives next door to them, for heaven's sake. He even dined with them sometimes, along with Allan and Caroline. It was like something out of a storybook."

"Sounds like it. He must've been pretty full of himself with all those connections." Abbey's voice softened with a playful lilt.

"Definitely," Victoria agreed. "He always tried to play it cool, like it wasn't a big deal, but you could see the pride in his eyes when he'd talk about college, especially when he brought up that famous actor from *World of Warriors*." She paused, letting the memory linger. "I'll never forget that day at Ohara's Jazz Bar. Sipping martinis, the music swirling around us, and Conor said, 'It's a shame we didn't meet earlier. You could've been my wife in the Hamptons, living the perfect life with our two daughters, Ava and Grace.'"

Abbey chuckled. "Oh, the dreamer. Were you ever tempted to play along?"

Victoria's smile faded slightly as she lost herself in the memory. "For a second, yeah. It was hard not to imagine that kind of life, the luxury and charm that surrounded him. It felt like we could've had it all. I was just walking into the piano bar, those red snakeskin stilettos clicking on the floor, and he was right there, standing next to me, all suave and gentlemanly. He touched my hand and said, 'Good evening, gorgeous.' Then, without missing a beat, he ordered me a dirty martini and the rest of the bar a round of drinks like it was nothing."

Abbey's voice turned thoughtful. "Sounds like he had a way of making you feel special, huh?"

Victoria nodded, her tone quieter now. "He did. He really did. It wasn't just about the money or the family name, it was the way he carried himself, that confidence. Class isn't something you learn; it's something you're born with. And Conor had it. It's the kind of thing I've never found in anyone else."

"You sure about that?" Abbey asked gently.

Victoria let out a sigh. "Maybe not. But Tony's... well, Tony's no Conor. He's like this game of cat and mouse, constantly toying with me, never making a move. It was all fireworks in the beginning, but it fizzled out. Every time we tried to make it work; it was like he forgot how to play the game. "He's in his own little world, thinking he's the main character, and I'm just the side story. I can't keep doing this. I deserve more than someone who doesn't even take the initiative." It's been years of him in and out of my life, and he's older now, as am I.

Abbey listened quietly, understanding the frustration in her cousin's voice. "But, V, what about now? Right now? If you were perfect enough for him back then, why wouldn't he see it now?"

Victoria paused; the weight of the question settled on her shoulders. "Maybe we were just each other's rebound, you know? Seeking love in all the wrong places, trying to fill a void that didn't need filling. But even so... I can't shake this feeling that I'm still drawn to him like a magnet. I keep wondering if there's a chance for something real. But the more I think about it, the more I realize I'm wasting my time in a story that's already played out. It's like a game of chess, and I'm just a pawn."

Abbey's voice softened with empathy. "You know what? It's okay to step away from the game, V. You're too good for this.

You deserve someone who knows what they want and isn't afraid to take the leap with you."

Victoria smiled faintly, grateful for her cousin's words. "Maybe you're right. Maybe it's time for me to stop being the backup plan and start thinking about what I really want... before it's too late."

"They're living together now, and he's been staying in the Canary Islands with her, I hear!" Abbey said, her voice was full of energy.

"That's awesome! But he still owes me that trip to Africa. I'm sure he'll be calling soon to catch me up. Oh, and guess what? We ran into each other about three months ago!" Victoria exclaimed.

"Wait, *where*? You never tell me anything!" Abbey leaned in, curious.

"Ah, I totally forgot to mention it! It was at the Gran Canaria Airport, of all places! And can you believe this—he wasn't even staying at my resort. He stayed at one of our competitors!" Victoria chuckled.

"I guess he didn't want to run into you, huh?" Abbey teased.

"Oh, trust me, he did! Too bad for him! He told me he'd just come back from a business trip to London. Get this: he stayed at the Four Seasons Canary Wharf in the *presidential suite*," Victoria said, her excitement growing.

"Wait, *how much* a night did he spend?" Abbey asked, her jaw dropping.

"$2,510 per night! It's east of London proper, super convenient to London City Airport. Conor could still meet his clients, review portfolios—the works! Plus, it's the *only* high-end hotel in the booming Canary Wharf area of London. Talk about top-tier!" Victoria said with a grin.

"Have you been there?" Abbey asked, eager to know more.

"Ha, you know I'm loyal to my family's resorts, but yeah, I've got to keep an eye on the competition. It's only a two-minute walk from the UK's new financial center, and it's *so* easy to get around with the gorgeous Jubilee Line Subway. The hotel's Quadrato Restaurant serves up amazing contemporary Italian, and there's a Holmes Health Club with this huge indoor pool. It's *incredible*," Victoria said, her excitement practically bursting through.

"What about the Victoria Suite in London? I hear you sold it," said Abbey.

"No loss—the Victoria Suite was ours, but my father gambled it away one drunken night to the Larsons over a poker game.

Strangely enough, they never renamed it, and interior designer Chrissie Fairlamb recently redecorated it," said Victoria.

"Sounds like Carlos needs to play poker with Mr. Larson again to win it back," said Abbey.

"No loss. You know I hate the cold weather," said Victoria. "I have to get ready for a meeting with the shareholders. Call me when you're in New York, and we'll meet up for dinner."

"Yes, I promise. Oh, and please give my warmest regards to Matt and tell him I said he shouldn't be shitting where he eats. Take it from me," said Victoria.

"Goodbye for now, cuz, and big hugs to Uncle Carlos from me," said Abbey.

"I'll be visiting him in the morning and will tell him. My mother would say that Carlos was well known for being a risk-taker in business and the way he lived life—with his superhuman strength. A thrill-seeking millionaire businessman, and he had the scars to prove it from many accidents throughout the years. He was once injured by closing train doors. Three broken ribs and still smiling. 'Love you too, cuz. Bye,'" said Victoria.

It was incredible that Carlos lived to talk about his last adventure, considering he should have died on his trip to Australia. He insisted on swimming with the sharks. His friend took him to a local dive shop, and a well-known man named Jake agreed to take him off the coast of Seal Island, the most dangerous shark-infested waters. The photos were absolutely amazing. His new wife had one blown up, and it now hangs in his office.

Only three days after Abbey called Victoria with the breaking news about Conor, he had called Victoria to mention he was engaged. Before saying hello, the sound of a hyper man's voice on the other end said, "I have gossip, Vic. It's excellent news. I am officially engaged to my soulmate. We are going to make beautiful babies," said Conor.

"Hi, O'Cryin', that is excellent news," said Victoria.

"Why do you still call me that?" asked Conor.

"Because you always sound as if you are crying. Therefore, I can't resist," said Victoria.

"You think you're always catchy with these nicknames for Dan the Man, Victor the Pilot, Crabby Abbey, Lame Jane? If only these people knew what you called them," said Conor.

"I won't apologize that you don't appreciate my humor. Listen, I must cut you short. It's been great reminiscing, but I have a meeting that I'm ten minutes late for—adiós, mi amigo," said Victoria.

"Wait, don't hang up. Can I set something up for you to meet my bride-to-be?" asked Conor.

"Why would I agree to that in God's name?" asked Victoria.

"She says she wants to meet you. I think you're her idol or something. She just read an article in *Time* magazine about your role at your father's office now that he had a near-death experience," said Conor.

"Another time, O'Cryin. I must hang up now," said Victoria.

"I heard about your father, and I am sorry. Is it true that the fucking shark bit his ass? What day is he leaving the hospital? No one from your office has called, not even my family or me, to inform us. I must be back at the bottom of your list," said Conor.

"Even with everything going on with my father, you still manage to be difficult. I'll be in touch," Victoria said, her tone sharp before the line went silent with a sharp click.

"Vickie? Vickie?" Conor muttered, momentarily stunned by her abruptness. He was taken aback that she'd hung up, though he couldn't deny that his timing with her had always been off. It was almost remarkable that he had been so successful as a hedge fund broker, considering how often he seemed to mismanage personal relationships. Maybe, he thought, she was the one that got away.

His mind drifted back to a particular moment in Key West — an evening under a full moon, the two of them alone in the Jacuzzi on a humid night. She had challenged him to swim with her, and without hesitation, Victoria had dropped her dress, playfully tossing her black lace bra and panties toward him. He recalled the way she appeared in the moonlight, her silhouette striking and undeniably alluring. The attraction he felt then was undeniable, but there was something more to it. It wasn't just desire; it was the kind of connection that lingered. Neither one of them told anyone about that evening, and Victoria and Conor never discussed it with each other, so they both thought there was no attraction.

The following day, Carlos was discharged from the hospital after a discussion with his doctor. They reached an agreement on the condition that he would be sent home accompanied by Nurse Annie. Victoria made daily visits to provide him with financial updates and ensured he was informed about any important news he had missed.

Victoria reluctantly decided it was time to return Conor's call. "I'm involved with my friend from 19P; she's a stunning redhead from Brooklyn," Conor said.

Victoria was taken aback. "You're actually dating someone from your building? Are you serious? I thought you were living in the Canary Islands—that's what Abbey told me. And are you engaged? What is wrong with you, Conor? You are such an asshole!" she asked, incredulous.

Conor responded with a hint of dismissal. "I am not a detestable person. Now you're sounding like a foul-mouthed Jersey girl," he said.

Victoria, clearly frustrated, pressed on. "You are the one who is vulgar, and you are annoying to me. Does she even know you're engaged, or is she simply unaware?"

Conor snapped back at Victoria, surprised that she was actually serious. "Yes, she knows, and it doesn't bother her. We're just having fun, and I can't resist her.

The exchange between Victoria and Conor lacked the usual lightheartedness she had remembered.

"It just happened," Conor explained. "I saw her at Cipriani's one night, and then I realized she looked familiar. I walked her home, and the rest was history. Now, she won't stop texting me. We have great textual chemistry."

He lay back, seemingly lost in thought, muttering, "I'm never drinking again."

Conor then continued, "Oh, you wouldn't believe it, my neighbors—let's just say they're very active right now, and their curtains are wide open, practically inviting everyone to watch."

Victoria, unimpressed, shot back. "You're still a peeping Tom in my eyes. Seriously, stop spying on your neighbors from the building across the way. And what's even worse is that you are now the guy with a side chick."

CHAPTER 11

BLACK SHEEP

Yuan, a direct descendant of the illustrious First Emperor Qin of China, was born into a lineage that traced its roots to the very heart of imperial power, making him, without question, royalty. Despite his vast influence, Yuan rarely wielded the weight of his ancestry, choosing instead to let his actions speak louder than his heritage. Yet, no one could deny the significance of his connection to the Great Wall of China or the legendary Terracotta Army, symbols of strength and eternity that echoed through the corridors of history.

At the tender age of seventeen, Aurora, driven by a thirst for a life beyond the confines of the Dharavi slums of India, sought refuge in a union with Yuan. He, with his royal lineage and unyielding resolve, brought her to the sprawling grounds of his ancestral estate. It was there, under the shade of ancient cherry blossoms, that they were wed in a ceremony of extraordinary grandeur—a union blessed by the elders and revered by all who witnessed it. The world had shifted for Aurora, and with it, the weight of history seemed to bear witness to the beginning of a new chapter.

Aurora later gave birth to Amida, the first child. At thirty-one, Amida was appointed Chief Financial Officer of the Zhang family's vast holdings, a position that created tension with Cash, the youngest sibling. Amida tragically passed away while on a business trip in Manila on August 8. Rumors swirled that the Chinese mafia was behind the accident. Mia, Amida's fiancée, remains in contact with Aurora, but the truth of that fateful night on the bridge may never be known.

The official report claimed that Amida overdosed on OxyContin, though some questioned the details, given that his body was found in pieces at Devil's Peak. Initially, the police suspected foul play, but the coroner ruled otherwise. The family was never satisfied with this explanation. Amida was an avid hiker, and his death didn't sit well with Yuan, who could not reconcile the circumstances. It wasn't until Dr. Yates convinced the family to accept the report that they moved forward. As Zenya scattered Amida's ashes from the cliff, a rusty nail fell from the urn—a peculiar and unsettling sign she couldn't ignore. In her heart, she still sensed his presence, as though he were watching over her. She couldn't help but question why the microchip hadn't led them to him sooner.

How was that possible, especially when she had been told they could live for eternity if they chose? Yet, she wasn't entirely convinced by her father Yuan's account of the tragic crash from their youth, when she was only about eight years old. The mention of Garnet and the concept of "Infinity" pursuing them left her skeptical. Perhaps now that she was older, Benji might finally be able to shed light on the mystery. There were still missing pieces to the story, and Zenya found herself yearning to understand what her father had burned that fateful day.

Amida had been engaged to Mia for just a month before his untimely death. Mia, forbidden to marry outside her Filipino heritage, had always been at odds with the Zhang family's expectations. Her father, a powerful tycoon, sat on the board of trustees at the corrupt Bank of the Philippine Islands.

Xenia, born on December 29, 1980, was given the nickname "Zenya" after a mix-up with her third-grade teacher's alternate spelling. The name itself, meaning "guest" or "stranger" in Greek, fit her well. Zenya often felt like an outsider in her own family, clinging to them for recognition but never truly feeling seen. Her hobbies—photography, martial arts, and writing—provided her with solace, though she always woke to the sounds of Mozart's *Fantasia in D Minor*, a haunting reminder of her father's music, which was no longer played by him.

Among the siblings, Zenya's twin, Cash, was the wealthiest, managing a vast portfolio while dividing his time between New York and France. He no longer had a residence in Asia but still maintained ties with the Hong Kong elite. Known for his hedonistic lifestyle and countless high-profile relationships, Cash was a notorious playboy. Yet, he remained committed to philanthropy, particularly to the poor in the Dharavi slums, where he helped build a pediatric hospital. His closest friend was Chen Li, a 30-year-old Chinese billionaire who founded A.I.ELITE, a company specializing in self-driving cars.

Yuan, though born into privilege, was a hard worker and ran the family's museum for much of his life. He had a deep passion for history and music, playing the piano daily. However, the family eventually learned that he was often lonely, drinking himself to sleep most nights. His marriage to Aurora had grown distant, especially after her infidelities with every gardener who passed through their estate, starting with Javier. Amida had once walked in on Aurora in the pool room with one of the gardeners, and her weak excuse—claiming he was simply massaging her back—left a deep wound in their relationship. That year, Amida left for college in Switzerland.

Amida's troubled teenage years were marked by multiple run-ins with the law, leading him to a treatment facility. It wasn't until after a year there that he began to turn his life around. He stopped drinking, and his newfound commitment to his fiancée, Mia, was solidified when he sent a photo of his first AA chip to Zenya. To celebrate, Zenya sent him and Mia a basket of bottled Diamond Water and round-trip tickets to Iceland's Mineral Spa.

Zenya had long been exposed to influential individuals, hoping they would help her advance in her career, only to realize that this wasn't the case. Her siblings squandered their inheritance and showed little interest in managing their finances. When Zenya decided to distance herself from the family, she did so with the understanding that they lacked the emotional maturity to have productive, intelligent conversations. She had spent too much time trying to navigate their toxic dynamics. On a summer evening at Devil's Peak, she made the choice to leave behind the family's dysfunction.

Family conflict, Zenya had come to understand, often arose from differing beliefs and unresolved issues. She had long stopped hoping for meaningful connections with her relatives, knowing they were incapable of offering the support and respect she desired. As a child, Zenya learned how to play hangman from her grandfather, Xian, who also taught her chess. But these games, symbolic of the way words could be twisted and used against her, mirrored her experiences in the family. For years, she had been subjected to backhanded comments and passive-aggressive remarks, the sting of which she had grown accustomed to.

Chia, her older sister, often spoke dismissively of Zenya, claiming that Zenya was selfish and self-centered. Chia had long taken the role of the family's golden child, while Zenya felt like the perpetual outcast. The tension only escalated as Zenya became more successful, traveling frequently and maintaining a busy lifestyle. She was grateful to have Victoria still in her life—a friendship and bond that would never be broken. They truly were sisters, despite being on different continents. Zenya had purchased a private plane and devoted her time to expanding the family's investments worldwide. Yet, despite her accomplishments, her family never seemed to recognize her efforts.

A few years ago, Zenya traveled to Dubai to celebrate her mother's birthday. During dinner at the renowned Ossiano, an elegant underwater Michelin-starred restaurant with Chef Grégoire Berger, Zenya arranged for a diver to hold up a "Happy Birthday Aurora" sign. However, the evening quickly turned sour when Aurora embarrassed everyone present. It became painfully clear that Aurora had long been the source of much of the family's discord. Zenya had always tried to distance herself from the drama, but after their final argument, she could no longer tolerate the situation. Hangman, she thought—G-A-M-E O-V-E-R. Aurora stood up and declared to the room that she enjoyed drinking, confronting the toxicity head-on.

The scene escalated for over ten minutes, with Aurora loudly berating the family, and at one point, even attempting to pull off Garnet's glasses. Zenya, who had quietly endured years of passive-aggressive comments and manipulation, finally decided it was enough. With Garnet, the matriarch, being the only force holding the family together, Zenya realized that the only way forward was to sever ties. She made her decision clear—this was the end of her relationship with Aurora. No more excuses, no more second chances.

Later, Zenya released a T-shirt line with the slogan "Keep Your Drama to Your Mama" through a social media app, symbolizing her resolve to leave the toxic family dynamics behind. Family gatherings were now solely driven by financial discussions and corporate agendas, with little attention paid to personal connections.

Zenya had no desire to revisit old conflicts, and when asked about her estrangement from her mother, she would simply say, "The lack of a relationship is between my mother and me. I don't want to bring you into it."

Zenya had long ago stopped seeking approval. She was content in her own skin, knowing she had accomplished everything on her own. Despite her family's rejection, she had never relied on their wealth or inheritance. She had worked tirelessly to build her own legacy, one rooted in her own strength and resilience.

For years, Zenya had been the scapegoat, the black sheep of the family. But now, she understood her worth. She had done the emotional work, healing from the wounds of her past. The freedom she felt in cutting ties with toxic family members was liberating. Zenya had learned to embrace the person she had become—a woman of strength, independence, and clarity.

Chia resided in Northern Hong Kong Island with her children, while Cash spent much of the year on various exotic islands, maintaining his jet-setting lifestyle. Meanwhile, his son Yang frequently traveled between Cyprus and Dubai with his young partner, Mohammed. Zenya, based in Sha Tin, Hong Kong, led a busy life, traveling monthly to oversee her properties and organizing numerous fundraisers around the globe.

Yuan divorced Aurora in favor of his girlfriend, unable to cope with the devastating loss of Amida. The grief proved overwhelming, and he ultimately chose to end the marriage.

CHAPTER 12

CASH ZHANG

Trent was 6'2", a former Olympic medalist rower. He had attended The University of Osijek in Croatia and was the 2016 Rio Silver medalist. His family owned the Joelle Hotel, where he would often be seen swimming laps in the pool or walking to the Adriatic Sea. Now a hedge fund manager at One World Global Firm, living in a stylish Manhattan brownstone with his live-in chef, the very handsome Mark Seaton, he had been writing a play about the secret lives of private chefs.

As Cash entered the room, Mark handed him a glass of 1995 Brunello. "Thanks, Mark," Cash said, shaking his hand as he winked at him. "Looking good, my friend," said Mark. Cash was wearing Florence red pants, a lime green T-shirt, an unbuttoned white collared long-sleeve shirt with the sleeves rolled up, and a red Hermès belt with matching loafers. Trent, walking out of his bedroom, approached Cash to hug him hello. Trent gave him a customary Croatian kiss three times on alternate cheeks.

"Welcome. How was your flight?" asked Trent.

"Funerals and family gatherings are constantly draining. Let's please keep my grandmother's funeral off-topic tonight. Seeing Chia and Zenya in tears was heartbreaking. Very seldom do you see those two in the same room these days," said Cash.

"Sure thing, Cash, and I am sorry about Garnet. I know how much she adored you, calling you her favorite when I used to see her in the Hamptons," said Trent.

"Hey, Mark, may I ask where everyone is? I see a few Lambos outside?" asked Trent.

"They are all up on the roof. Dinner will be at 7 p.m.," said Mark.

"Cash, my man, we haven't seen you since last summer in France on your yacht. What an epic party that was," said Chen Li.

"Yes, that was a memorable day. Oh, and the Russian strippers would not leave the next morning," said Cash.

"How's your son, Yang? Is he still with that Lebanese guy, Mohammed? I remember your son telling us he was flying back and forth from Cyprus to Dubai to visit him?" asked Trent.

"No, man. Yang and Mohammed broke up. Just another gold digger. His true colors came out, and I can't stand to watch him follow in my footsteps," said Cash.

"What exactly does Mohammed do for work?" asked Oscar.

"He was the programmer and gatekeeper of several porn sites, but now we think he works for the government. My son never cared for his family. Mohammed never wanted his picture taken, stating that he needed to return to the Keto diet to get back his lean six-pack abs. He would explain why he wasn't speaking to his mother because she never shed a tear at his father's funeral," said Cash.

"Well, he's a cool dude and will find the right one, like I did with my partner Oscar here," said Javier, showing a sign of love by squeezing the back of his neck.

"Now that we are all caught up on my family drama, why don't we talk about our next business venture?" said Cash. They shared a few more laughs before dinner, while drinking the rest of the '95 Brunello.

"You think Carlos Holdings' stock will continue to plummet as his presence fades? I hear he is not well these days," said Chen Li.

"All I know is my family continues to sink money into Carlos's Holdings. That man will outlive all of us, and Victoria is still best friends with my sister Zenya. Loyal to the bone, those girls," said Cash.

Trent and Victoria had a summer fling a few years back while in the Hamptons after a diving trip with Carlos, but nothing ever came of it. "Victoria won't ever return my calls. She responds via text with a one-liner. How is she doing these days?" asked Trent.

"Working hard, as usual. You know her work ethic more than any of us, Trent. No more carefree days in the Maldives," said Cash.

"When have you seen her last?" asked Trent.

"Victoria will be making an appearance at my niece's wedding. I saw her at a Southampton party. She was visiting Zenya, and they stayed at Grandmother Garnet's house. Victoria looked amazing, and Conor McAdams, that lucky bastard, is still around," said Cash. "I am getting hard just thinking about her. She can throw some money my way anytime."

"Chen Li, a Chinese billionaire who founded A.I.ELITE, Inc., Hollywood's go-to man for futuristic cars that drive themselves, had his younger girlfriend standing in the corner, caressing herself while watching the sunset."

"The upside of going to the Hamptons this weekend is that Victoria is throwing a party at Red Elephant. The downside is that she's inviting my ex," said Trent.

"Some of those Hamptons parties are for hunting elephants, and McAdams stays away from the pikers—well, and the swinging dicks, also. Both brothers seem to think they are above all that, and perhaps that is why everyone loves these two, including my sister Zenya. She has always liked John but won't tell Victoria that," said Cash.

Trent says, "Well, Conor doesn't deserve Victoria, and he is always flirting with Zenya. Is that to upset Victoria, you think?" asked Trent.

Carlos shuts down every relationship that Victoria has, so clearly, obviously, we know Victoria is never going to end up with either of them. Zenya will need to figure this out on her own; I already told my sister I am not getting in the middle of her and Victoria.

"It's time to light up the night with fireworks and shots!" said Chen Li, his voice full of energy as he raised his glass. The crew had just wrapped up an unforgettable evening—reminiscing with old friends, swapping next-level ideas for the upcoming angel investors meeting, and living like only billionaires do. They were all part of that exclusive 5AM club, where ambition never sleeps, and the champagne never runs dry. The energy was electric, but as always, the party was about to hit its final lap.

"Mark, that meal was nothing short of a masterpiece," Cash said, tipping his glass toward the chef. "And Trenton, man, thank you for an incredible night. But I've got to bounce—stay sharp, stay healthy." With a smile, Cash made his exit, the night still young and the possibilities endless.

CHAPTER 13

VICTORIA DEROSSI

Victoria met her high school friend Anna out on Las Olas Boulevard. Victoria had decided to take a taxi up the street, as she was only living a few blocks east on Hendricks Isle, just off the main road of Las Olas, known as the jewel of Fort Lauderdale. They have everything for a fantastic evening out or even a leisurely day while docking at the Port of Everglades to go window-shopping and brunching at one of many romantic sidewalk cafes.

Anna's co-worker introduced Stuart to Victoria. They met at the Porsche dealership about five years ago, and she had been playing cupid all these years. Finally, Victoria took the time to meet Stuart, although she had never dated a Jewish person.

Catholicism had been important to her as a child, and now as a young adult, she was practicing Buddhism. Some would say she was spiritual. They enjoyed the live music at Mango's and ordered a few different appetizers in the lounge. Anna gave a hug to Victoria and Stuart. "I'll see you when I see you," said Anna, wanting to leave them alone as she went to the ladies' room. Victoria followed and said, "Hey, Anna, I will call it a night." Stuart walked the girls to the front entrance, where he asked Victoria if she would like to meet him for sushi the next night.

A few days before she had to report back to work to her father's resort, Victoria kindly accepted, thinking to herself that everyone was looking for love. Knowing Tony would be in town this week, Victoria did not want to make plans, plus there was no sexual chemistry with Stuart. She didn't want to hurt his feelings or disappoint Anna.

The following day, Victoria phoned Stuart. "Sorry, I need to cancel. Something came up," said Victoria.

"What may I ask why?" said Stuart.

"I have to watch my sister's kids," said Victoria.

"Oh, damn, I bought you a gift," said Stuart.

"A gift? That's quick. You just met me last night, and you bought me a gift?" said Victoria as she hugged him.

"Roses for a beautiful lady," said Stuart. She thought how sweet it was that she had been dating the pilot for months, and he had yet to spend money on her for roses or even a romantic dinner.

Men are strange. In recent conversations with Brett, he explained that there are women men are attracted to; however, these are the women that are not interesting to him. Then there are those lady friends with whom men have beautiful relationships, but there is no attraction. Victoria knew she had been feeling this way for her pilot friend for quite some time now. She was attracted to him unconditionally, making love to him three times a day without hesitation, but only to come to the realization that she had absolutely nothing in common with him.

She even told him jokingly that she would give him a job on her private jet when she bought another resort. They had different interests. Thank God he could find employment for a charter Part 91 airline. He hated the Gulfstream, missing the commercial planes. He was miserable, with low self-esteem now. Many would think they could find another aviation job, but he had changed, and he was now a man back in his cave.

He cannot enjoy a cocktail or even kick back and order a bottle of wine. The last time he was in town, she mentioned picking up a bottle of wine and taking a walk on the beach, but he had to say that he was on a budget and would remain this way until he gets that left seat salary. Most women these days demand to be taken out to dinner, wine and dined, perhaps even 69-ed, but getting the milk for free. Why bother to be pretentious and wine and dine with someone? That was his motto. Maybe things will change when he is making $200,000 annually. Anthony collects that in rent from his tenants, not to mention his directors' salary at the resort, which pays six figures.

Victoria had a busy day at work today, putting out many fires. Midday, she received a call from her stepmother Olivia that her father had another heart attack and was in the hospital. Saddened by the news, the nervous daughter hung up and handed the valet her ticket. As she sat in the red McLaren 720S Spider, she caught some attention from the bystanders. Going well above the speed limit to the hospital with the wind in her hair, she checked her voicemail messages. "Victoria, I am sorry I missed you. I wanted to let you know I am traveling to Hawaii at the end of the month and would love it if you would join me," said Anthony.

At the hospital, Victoria was crying because her father was still not awake, and she was all alone without her sister Valentina. She needed to decide. Taking a walk to calm her nerves, Victoria stopped to purchase a cup of coffee and chatted with Carlos's cardiologist, Dr. Moffitt, about her father's worsening condition. He explained to her the procedure for pig heart valve replacement, and she would have to choose whether to use a biological or mechanical valve to replace the diseased valve.

"Dr. Moffitt, do you have a preference or more experience with one or the other?" asked Victoria.

Dr. Moffitt was leaning up against the cafeteria door with one foot on the wall. He was a young doctor in his forties, one of the best cardiologists in the U.S.

"The first and foremost benefit of pig heart transplant surgery is that Carlos will not need to take blood-thinning medicines. I know he leans more toward the holistic side, and he is as active as any thirty-year-old. Honey, your father will be fine. Dr. Yates has just landed on the hospital rooftop heliport. He will discuss this procedure further with you. Ask all your questions and decide, and then we can review the DNR. You know your father's desire to live a healthy lifestyle, and he will be just fine." Dr. Moffitt smiled and walked over to the elevator to greet Dr. Yates. It was a nail-biter, but Victoria knew Carlos would approve the replacement surgery. Victoria agreed if the doctor could assure her it wouldn't interfere with the blood flow of his human body.

She phoned Valentina, who was in the Swiss Alps, and her only question was how long her father could live with it. Dr. Yates advised about fifteen to seventeen years.

Later that night, after she returned home, she took a hot bath. Anthony Donochello had called. "Hi, can you hold a moment? I just am getting out of the tub," said Victoria.

"Now, don't excite me," said Anthony.

"Hello, how are you?" asked Victoria.

"What is wrong, honey? Is this a bad time?" asked Anthony.

"Sorry I never returned your call. My father is back in the hospital. I feel very numb," said Victoria.

"What does his doctor say?" asked Anthony.

"It is not good, and he is still in critical condition; I had to leave. Valentina is in Switzerland with the UNESCO group, and my stepmother is with him now," said Victoria.

"He will pull through. He is one tough man. You know I just saw him last week. He flew in from Fiji. He had this deep, dark golden tan and said he played a few rounds of golf with his buddies that morning. I even joked with him, saying that he had a Hamilton tan. Carlos said, 'Now-now, don't offend me. The kids from Victoria's school called me Randy Garcia and not Hamilton.' Your dad is an amazing, jovial person. He is going to pull through this," said Anthony.

"I hope he pulls through. Your words to God's ears. Tell me about your award," said Victoria.

"Well, first off, can you come with me? Hawaii would be better with you?" asked Anthony.

"How about a rain check?" said Victoria. "I need to take a trip back to Florida and check on some of my properties. How about dinner soon before someone new falls in love with you again and beats me to it?" said Anthony.

How sweet, she thought, if she could only trust him. Here was a guy who never pursued her since he worked at her family's company, always fearful that he would lose his job and heart, since the rumor was that Victoria had a fiancé. Anthony may play the shy act, but he didn't want to *shit* where he ate or, in his case, some might say, dip his pen in the company ink.

Victoria never dated anyone at the resort, and now she was acting president while her father was in the hospital. She was his boss no matter what, and she didn't want to play with his emotions. The fact was that Anthony knew more about her and her family, interests, and dislikes than her main squeeze, Victor, of five months. Part of the pursuit was a common interest, and much sexual texting happened while he was out of town, but there was a disconnect with him these days, and she had to end it with Victor. Soon he would need to be on call for four weeks, living every other month in Wyoming, and Vickie hated cold weather.

"I look forward to seeing you, but I am a little distracted right now between my father in the hospital and the merger at the company," said Victoria.

"I can't lose my opportunity again, and you owe me a date—Dolce dormie. I will keep Carlos in my prayers. Let me know if anything changes. Buon Notte," said Anthony.

The following day, Victoria walked into Carlos's private room in the east wing, and to her surprise, he was already awake and gave her the thumbs-up gesture from his hospital bed.

"Dad, how are you feeling?" asked Victoria, as Dr. Yates and Dr. Moffitt simultaneously entered the room.

"I feel fantastic and have already been walking the hallways. Thanks to my bright doctors and nurses, I will be ready to dive later today. Wheels up at noon," said Carlos.

"Victoria, your father is a jokester," said Dr. Moffitt as he reached over to hug her.

"Thank you both for helping my father. Our family will forever be indebted to you both," said Victoria.

The nurse walked in, bringing another get-well balloon and flowers for Carlos. She sat the vase on the table beside him and then fluffed his pillows. She grabbed a piece of chocolate as she walked out the door. Victoria sat in the chair next to her father as she reached into her jacket pocket to grab her vibrating cell phone. It was Valentina calling from Switzerland to inquire how he was doing.

Smiling, Victoria said, "Ask him for yourself," and handed the phone to Carlos.

"Hi, pops I am so happy to hear your voice. Mom sends her love," said Valentina.

"Now, tell Sonia I am fine. She is not getting all my money today. It would be better if you were here with your sister and Olivia and me," said Carlos.

"I am coming to see you soon, I promise, just as soon as I can get off from work. I love you, Pops," said Valentina.

"Bye, honey. Love you too, and please tell Sonia not to worry about me," said Carlos as he handed the phone back to Victoria.

CHAPTER 14

ZHANG FAMILY HOLDINGS

Zhang Family Holdings housed the most prominent corporate office in Southeast Asia and contained a two-story shopping mall and a gym. The twenty-story corporate office building in Hong Kong's downtown financial district included a private home consisting of five floors, with a private helipad on the roof reserved just for the Zhangs and several infinity outdoor pools. Shareholders and clients stayed on the residence side of the building while traveling on business. Asia's most important financial center housed around 3.5 million people, and security always accompanied the family.

John Paul McAdams III daydreamed of seeing her again in those Christian Louboutin red bottoms with the spikes—the ones he had bought her. A photo of the executive's last annual gala dinner sat on his desk; Zenya was wearing a Hermès red silk blouse and a black skirt. It was her gentle touch he missed most.

Using sex as power, she thought, might guarantee divorce, as most men didn't want a girlfriend. They love the attraction of the sneaky cat and mouse. Why, she wondered, nodding her head as he had texted her, "Where are you?" She tried not to get distracted while driving the sports car higher up the parking garage to find her reserved parking spot, knowing she was late for that 10:00 a.m. meeting. John would always watch to see when she was entering the building. Zenya sometimes felt as if surveillance had been monitoring her every action to gather information to give John. The staff all called him J.P., not to confuse him with his father.

The first time he made a pass at her, they just hugged, and Zenya was worried, looking around to make sure that nobody saw. Then, it became more open and obvious—his affection for her in the middle of the workday. That "don't bite the apple" sort of theory—as in Adam and Eve. Temptation, as if it was cat and mouse. On this day, she couldn't find him. Instead, she encountered a younger woman, dressed the same, in her twenties with long brown hair. Zenya overheard her asking the receptionist where the restroom was.

Following this gorgeous twenty-something-year-old purposely bumping into her, she said, "Oh hello, I know you, Zenya. I am Sasha." It turns out she was a friend of Larson's son. "You appear to be lost. Are you looking for someone?" The young girl said, "It is just so hard to meet a man here." It was a two-story shopping mall, a maze if you do not read the signage.

Zenya asked, "Well, what is your type of guy?" Sasha looked around the center and said, "I don't know; a fit man with a six-pack would be great." Zenya replied, "Young or old men?" The young, innocent girl laughed. "No, definitely young. (chuckling) An old man is gross," said Sasha.

They walked towards the gym, and Zenya said, "Now, my friend, this is where you will meet that 25-year-old inside this gym. Perhaps he works here." She knew that Larson's son, Brian, was working that day, and he was quite the eye candy.

Now, back to the cat-and-mouse game to find J.P. Today, she knew he had flown in the evening prior for a business meeting with the shareholders. She wanted him, and they hadn't gone that far yet—just casual fondling. The excitement was now enticing, especially because the divorce proceedings, he said, were finally coming to fruition. Zenya opened the glass conference room door, smiling at the others around the table as she pulled out the only available chair next to J.P.

When the situation began, we were ramping up sales with the spending bill while it took off. We see that soften in preparations for service going to the max, and it will be pushed out in a few years, if you will, at a normalized 2022 level. It is a multi-year recovery, which applies to both the portfolio and buy-and-hold sides.

"Zenya, please go ahead."

"Good morning. Any way to think about the cost analysis vs. the CEO announcement? The broadening across the company, if you look at the tally today, shows short-term bias, stability, and a solid foundation that Marcella and I will be working with during the coming weeks. We will transition to a more permanent position with John in charge of our America office. We need to work on the changes required for the length of recovery. We will be leading the $3 billion of cash to make more of them permanent, recognizing the cost side in some of the work of the capital—a 25% reduction. By no means are these headlines today the end. It is very much a work in progress."

"We think the $20 million came in at the perfect time. Does it sit on the balance sheet for the year, or can we start to parse it out to some of the debts, if you can manage it? It did come at a good time. That is why we want to take the market risk off the table," said Zenya.

"Anything you want to add about liquidity vs. leverage?" said Lawrence, a shareholder seated at the end of the table.

"We under-quartered with $40 million cash, and we were down to $13 billion in maturities in total capital. $20 billion in line of credit, which is good. A high level of money to the max. We will prudently manage the funds during this time. J.P. from Morgan Stanley, has the impact of retirements made a U-shape? Is there a natural lag when spenders get back out?"

"Certainly, J.P., the group is well-versed in the subject," said Zenya. The meeting went on for another hour.

When the news of a one-world currency of Bitcoin conversions in the banking system took over, most civilians were left with less than one hundred dollars in their accounts as all monetary funds, including stock market shares, were converted into the popular digital coin called Devil Coin. Money market accounts, 401(k) accounts, and families were all wiped clean and wholly blindsided with no warning.

Families ready to retire were stripped clean of any future retirement plans. Social Security ended abruptly, and veterans stopped receiving the monthly checks that they lived off. Some had worked forty years in unions awaiting that big payout of investment stock funds. Sadly, it never happened. The elite corporations took it all to divvy up among themselves and then paid China what was owed to them ever since the Widen and Karris Presidency. It was a fool's game with very few winners.

Everyone's life now felt somewhat distorted from the truth, as if they were living out some scene in a communist movie. It was not much better for the one percentile. Families witnessed loved ones dragged out of bed with nothing more than the shirts on their backs—some even naked. America was now just like any third-world country. No more freedom, just rules and one world order with a one-world global currency.

It was the weekend, and she slept in after her hellacious week in the office. Tossing and turning in bed, waking to see 8:08 a.m. flashing on the wall clock—the electricity must have gone off for a moment. She had a frightening dream that included the president of the United States signing a bill giving China ownership of 50 states and 14 territories, including a federal district and some of the island nations, many of which included an expensive luxury DeRossi Resort. As she turned, she noticed the barge rope was loose and starting to pull away from the sand. She did not want to float further into the ocean. The girl jumped off, and her toes touched the sand. She turned her back to look up one last time, and to her surprise, he was right there beside her.

Wearing a pair of jeans, shirtless, with six-pack abs and a small cross and bow-and-arrow tattoo on his right shoulder with the words "LOLA," he had blonde, wavy hair and whispered to her, "You are going up tomorrow, I hear," said the warrior. In all the dreams, her warrior never conversed in English with her.

"You finally made it. How do you feel now that you will soon be reunited with your family?" said the warrior. Speechless, the girl said nothing and woke up to the blinking 8:08 a.m. on the wall clock. She clicked the white button on the shades remote control to ensure she wasn't still in her crazy dream. She was silently lying in her bed, wondering what the hell that dream meant. She wondered if the warrior represented John, figuring it may be time to pull out those old childhood journals to dissect the dreams she had written down.

Zenya couldn't help but feel a flutter in her chest whenever she saw John. There was something about him that captivated her—his effortless charm, the depth in his eyes, and, above all, his intelligence. She found herself lost in admiration for him more often than she'd like to admit, wondering what made him so different from his brother Conor. While Conor had his own appeal, John had a gentleness, a kindness, that made him stand out in her heart.

Each conversation with him left her feeling warm, as if he had a way of seeing the world that no one else did. She marveled at how effortlessly he spoke, how every word seemed to carry meaning. She couldn't help but think about him, her thoughts always returning to his soft smile and the way he listened so intently.

Why was he so much more thoughtful, more patient than Conor? It was a question that lingered in her mind, but she didn't mind. The mystery only made her more curious—and more drawn to him. There was something deeply romantic in the way he made her feel seen, understood, and cherished in ways she never imagined.

CHAPTER 15

MARKET PLUMMETS

It was a Friday afternoon when the market was dropping due to the sudden death of Carlos Holdings, a U.S. billionaire who had been in and out of the hospital the past few years. Another billionaire, Asian Zenya Zhang, became best friends with his daughter, Victoria, a teenage model for the St. John clothing line. She is often photographed in St. John and Chanel suits, as seen on page six. Zenya could not believe Carlos was gone. He had always been a second father to her. He died mysteriously from a brain aneurysm in South Asia while diving in the Maldives. Some conspiracy theorists say it was the vaccine jab.

Just the week prior, Victoria explained to Zenya that she would have to return her call later in the day. Victoria was in New York, accompanying Carlos for his annual EKG at New York-Presbyterian Hospital-Columbia before going to the Maldives. She later reported to Zenya that the Italian stallion had a clean bill of health and could continue doing all the things he loved, such as diving. He was in great shape at 64 and sexy as ever to his new trophy wife, Olivia. Always more of a friend than a father. Victoria returned Zenya's call to say that they were off to the Maldives—"Come and join us anytime and bring Cash and Trent." Nobody believed he was gone.

These funerals of high-profile people cost millions of dollars to the authorities. However, they deserve a royal and memorable goodbye. Carlos was on a well-deserved vacation on his private yacht while also spending time in his Reval Blanch's overwater estate. It was an architectural masterpiece, and Zenya loved to visit but couldn't make it this time. Half of the home is underwater, making it a diver's delight.

OBITUARY

Carlos DeRossi met Jesus face to face on January 9, surrounded by his family in the Maldives. He was born in Viareggio, Italy, on August 8, 1957. He was preceded in death by his parents, Santiago DeRossi and Sofia Rose Cortez-DeRossi, and his baby brother, Sebastián. Carlos was a real estate tycoon for 34 years and specialized in luxury resorts. Admired and respected by his peers, who considered him one of the most pleasing investors in the world, he loved Jesus, his family, his profession, and his country. Carlos was a true gentleman and a gentle giant. Carlos DeRossi is survived by his wife, Olivia; ex-wife, Sonia; two daughters, Victoria and Valentina; and husband, Dr. Sebastian Sorrella. He is survived by three grandchildren, Victor, Vanessa, and Valeria. He is also survived by six siblings: Nicolás, Isabella, Matteo, Diego, Luciana, and Camila, along with numerous nieces, nephews, and cousins.

Carlos's life will be celebrated on January 11 at 2 p.m. at Fellowship Bible Church, Rangali Island (masks required), with private interment at Lockshire's Gardens. For those who cannot attend, a live stream will be available at live.fellowship.maldives.org. To place an online tribute, visit www.lockshire.carlos.com.

Instead of flowers, the family requests memorial donations in his honor to the Shriners Heart Foundation, 699 Saturn Ave.,

NW, Las Vegas, NV 24016. Online condolences may be shared with the family at www.oaksobits.com.

Published January 9, 2021, Wall Street Journal

~~~~~~~~~~~~~~~~~~~~~~~~~~~~~~~~~~

Victoria's father had suffered two heart attacks while they were living in Hong Kong. All the traveling caused a strain on his marriage to Sonia. They divorced, and he was quite a playboy until he remarried his much younger secretary, Olivia. Victoria was

black suits, his tan complexion resembled the famous American actor, Randy Garcia.

All the kids had a crush on him back in the day, saying he was fun to be around and had a sleek black Porsche before upgrading to the NIO Owl. Carlos was a true car enthusiast, always talking shop about his latest rides. One night, after a

student-teacher meeting, he took a few of the kids for ice cream, cruising through the streets with the engine purring, like a man who truly appreciated the thrill of the drive.

The kids piled into the back seat, and Carlos would say, "Hold on, kids," as he sped down the empty street at 90 mph. He was often photographed boarding his private plane. Victoria and Zenya first met when they were students in Hong Kong and again in the Hamptons, solidifying the strong bond between two friends across the globe. Yet, twenty years later, they remained best friends. The families were both well-connected globally, and the girls became roommates while attending preparatory school in Switzerland. It's too bad Carlos yanked her out early to be with him in Palm Beach. Zenya always knew Cash liked Victoria, and she often thought about a fun time when they spent spring break at Carlos's resort in Fiji. That was where the girls learned how to dive. Cash always had a crush on Victoria, and even today, she still calls him "Mr. Smutty."

Years later, Zenya and Cash made it a tradition to embark on an annual trip to the Maldives, where they'd dive alongside Carlos. It was during one of these trips that Victoria first crossed paths with Trent, much to Cash's dismay—he never thought he measured up to Victoria's standards. But despite the drama, their shared passion for adventure never wavered. Swimming with the sharks remained their ultimate thrill, an unforgettable experience year after year.

Still in utter disbelief, the news hit like a thunderclap during the 5:00 p.m. media briefing, leaving everyone in the room stunned. The muted TV at the bar suddenly caught everyone's attention, the gravity of the moment sinking in. Zenya, out with colleagues at a local restaurant that had reserved a table for them, couldn't help but feel the weight of it all. It was a place they'd frequented, where they'd enjoyed the serene beauty of the 10-minute light show every Friday. But tonight, it was different. The usual buzz at the Sky Bar & Cafe was replaced with a heavy silence, the reality of Carlos's death still hard to process.

CHAPTER 16

BADASS BITCHES

VICTORIA

Victoria was one lucky lady, now running the family company in Las Vegas independently after her father passed away that horrible day. What a shame, especially since Carlos had made such a quick recovery, until fate intervened. If only he had had a premonition—or a dream—something that might have changed his mind that day.

Now, four months later, she found herself looking back, wondering: If she could see him just one more time, what would she say? She would tell him how much she loved and admired him, and most importantly, that she forgave him for not making things work out with her mother, Sonia. At times, Victoria wondered if this had been the reason she could never fully commit to anyone. Maybe she feared they would get bored and leave, just like her father had.

She'd sworn to herself at twelve years old, sitting at her bedroom desk, writing in her diary, that she would never be a needy woman who relied on a man to support her. Victoria had always wanted to marry—sure, she thought she'd have a child or two one day. It didn't have to be that picture-perfect white picket fence, just a happy marriage with children would suffice.

At fifteen, living with her mother, she still spent time back and forth between homes, splitting her time between her mother's house and Carlos's. Victoria gravitated more toward Carlos, wanting to stay in Hong Kong. Her sister Valentina, two years older and tired of the family drama, had moved to New York for college. For the most part, Victoria had felt like an only child. When her mom remarried, they'd lived between homes in Palm Beach and Manhattan, but the house in the Hamptons was still shared with Carlos and Olivia. Sonia had married a retired businessman who'd sold his company for a fortune in the mid-nineties. With his various small investments, he could work from anywhere, allowing them to move between homes, travel overseas, and send Victoria to boarding school, where she met Zenya.

Victoria knew her clock was ticking, but she had responsibilities—more now than ever. Not just as the Vice President on paper, but as the CEO of the Resort powerhouse. She knew Carlos was watching from above, and she had to make him proud. It was all she knew.

Valentina never got involved in the family business. Instead, she'd become a criminal lawyer in Italy, married to a cardiovascular surgeon with three children, all in private school. One of her daughters had even interned at a London resort—until Carlos lost it all to gambling.

Anthony kept calling, and she knew Victoria Donochello had a nice ring to it. She sometimes wondered why women often say their boyfriend's last name out loud, repeating it like it meant something. Maybe it's the flow. Valentina was lucky—she hadn't taken her husband's surname when she married in Italy. They don't do that there.

Anthony had lived the high life, partied, and achieved a string of top sales awards, but there was still that perfect woman missing from his life. He wasn't whole, he said, until he found her and started a family. Maybe Victoria was the one. He was flying into Vegas from Nashville on Friday to see if the chemistry between them could spark.

Victoria spent most of her time in Vegas now, living on-site at the resort. Anthony was up for a raise and possibly even interested in managing the resort.

Carlos would smile from above, happy to see these two finally come together. Anthony and Carlos had shared a special bond—a father-son type of connection. Perhaps that was why Victoria never got too close to Anthony; she knew the bond between him and her father was tight. The Donochellos owned the largest privately-owned sanitation company in North America, providing temporary traffic control since 1970. They had a quiet role in New York's underground dealings, ensuring the silence of mafia activities. Meetings often took place at the Caputo family home, near Vagen Ranch Road's private landing strip.

Quietly in and out, they'd plan their next moves. Now, living between a condo in Las Olas, downtown Fort Lauderdale, and the Vegas Resort, Victoria was beginning to feel more at peace. At least her shoes were enjoying the house in Florida that Carlos had gifted to her after graduation. She often flew back and forth on Victor's charter plane to Vegas. It was exciting when she saw him, looking handsome in his pilot uniform. Of course, he couldn't take a break from his job to be with her the way she wanted, but she had been holding out for weeks.

Victor had girlfriends—probably in every city—but she didn't care. She knew how she felt when she was with him. That night, feeling particularly bold, she hiked up her skirt, walked into the cockpit, and took him right there in front of the first officer. He excused himself quickly, leaving them alone.

Victor had struggled to get where he was after graduating from Embry. He'd tried everything—wasting time on failed businesses like wave runner rentals and vending machines, constantly chasing the next big deal. It wasn't until he was furloughed by the airline that he started selling cars.

Poor guy. He'd knocked on doors at the executive airport, missing that left seat and the salary that went with it.

Mesmerized by his touch, Victoria found peace in his arms. Knowing how much he adored her changed how she felt about him. They never exchanged "I love you"s, but she felt something deeper.

At times, she wondered if it was just about good sex. After all, they ran in different circles, and she was practically his boss, paying him to fly her around. He should've been nothing more than a glorified chauffeur.

She'd just called off her engagement to Martin, not ready to take that next step with Victor either. A part of her felt the weight of it all—wondering if she'd ever find a real, loving, trustworthy relationship. But she also felt a strange thrill, like maybe if she could hold out just a little longer, Anthony would find someone else to chase. Her father had always been there, her best friend, the one who saw through the bullshit and told her the truth about the men she picked. Now, with him gone, she felt lost in a way she couldn't quite explain. Who would tell her the truth now? Was she just doomed to stumble through, chasing something she wasn't even sure she could find anymore?

The truth was, Victoria excelled at everything—except love. She was terrified of it, pushing everyone away before they could get too close. She used to believe in love at first sight, in those perfect, fairy-tale relationships. But now? Now it all felt like a lie. A cruel, never-ending story where the girl meets the guy, falls in love, and then gets left behind for someone younger, thinner, sexier. It was always the same, and she was tired of waiting for a happy ending that never came.

Ten years, maybe even twenty years of marriage, and that husband would be chasing every skirt in a twenty-mile radius, including those twenty years younger. It was a losing battle.

Victoria had a nine-a.m. meeting with her accountant, Randall Rodriguez, to go over her father's will. She had already heard it once, when the family had gathered. Now, everyone knew she was acting CEO of Carlos Holdings. The staff had always known she would take over one day. But she was tired of reviewing the fine print. Losing her father was hard enough.

As she sat in the accountant's office, sipping her black coffee, she daydreamed about vacations—diving off the coast of Fiji. How would it feel to dive there now, without her dad?

With a spark in her eyes and a grin spreading across her face, she leaned forward and whispered, "I know exactly what I'm going to do in honor of Carlos. I'm opening a brand-new resort in Fiji—just like the Bellagio in Vegas." The idea electrified her, fueling a rush of excitement that stirred something deep inside. This was the next big move. And she couldn't wait to make it happen.

She loved the attention Victor gave her. He would call her "Victoria Donochello" with such confidence, as if the name fit her perfectly. He often repeated that she was his type—confident and sexy. She knew she was a fool not to be attracted to him.

But it was time for her to take a risk. No more yesterday, no more selfish men in her life who didn't care. They all had careers and lives. If her lover couldn't take five minutes out of his sleep time to say he missed her, then he wasn't the one for her.

ZENYA

It was Sunday morning, and Zenya's phone rang. She glanced at the clock—6 a.m.? Who would be calling this early? Before she could even greet her, a tired but familiar voice crackled through the line. "Hello, daughter, it's your mother, Aurora. Remember me?"

"Mom! Hi! How are you?" Zenya asked, still shaking off sleep. "I meant to call you. Is everything okay?"

"Life is peachy," Aurora replied, as though it were an understatement. "But have you seen the pictures of your niece's wedding dress?"

Zenya blinked in confusion. "Wedding dress? What wedding dress?"

"Chia posted a bunch of photos on social media. Your niece, Sukhi, has chosen her dress!" Aurora said with evident excitement.

Zenya sighed, a little annoyed. "I don't do social media, Mom. I had no idea they were even shopping for a wedding dress this weekend."

Blindsided again. She had missed yet another key moment in her niece's life, a moment that should have been shared with her as an aunt, as a sister.

"When was the last time you saw them, Zenya?" Aurora pressed.

"Just this past Saturday. We went on a hike near my house," Zenya replied with a touch of sarcasm. "Bye, mother, I need my sleep. Thanks for the update."

Zenya hung up, frustrated, but her mind started racing. The traditions, the excitement of family milestones—she felt like she was always just out of reach. In the Zhang family, the aunt was expected to cover the cost of the wedding dress. It was a *big* moment—the dress shopping, the cheers, the champagne toast, the celebratory dinner at L'Atelier de Joël Robuchon, where they would sit at the bar counter and watch the chefs work their culinary magic. All of it was *supposed* to be hers to share.

But once again, Zenya was left on the outside, excluded from an event she should have been a part of, left to watch through the lens of social media instead of real life. Her family's gatherings were always punctuated by those same old feelings of being an outcast, the black sheep, the one who was never truly included.

She remembered the family brunches, New Year's parties, all the posts about family and love. But no invitations for Zenya. Her friends, especially the ones close by in Asia, had been saying for months that something was off—that Chia had something against her. And honestly? Maybe they were right. Zenya had never quite understood why, despite living so close, she and her sister had never connected. It must be all that new wealth, that sense of distance between them all.

Zenya's thoughts swirled with the painful realization that, despite being labeled altruistic, she had always been the odd one out. Chia had kept her kids isolated from the rest of the family, with *her* controlling every move they made. Zenya couldn't help but think of all the outings she had been excluded from. Family events that, in a healthy dynamic, would have included everyone—the aunt, the cousins, and the godmother. Yet here she was, alone, always hearing about these moments secondhand, through whispers and social media posts.

It is almost 6:10 a.m. now. Zenya couldn't sleep on it. She grabbed her keys, threw her hair into a ponytail, and slammed the door behind her, feeling a rush of energy flooding her system. *Selamat pagi, Miss Zenya*, the bellman greeted her, but she couldn't hear him through the earbuds as Eminem's "Lose Yourself" blared in her ears, pumping her up.

She was ready to take on the world, but it was the world of her family that seemed to leave her behind. Chia, living carefree, constantly avoiding connection. Zenya, the one who tried to be the good daughter, the good aunt, the good sister—yet always ended up on the periphery. Even Victoria, her best friend, had noticed the dysfunction, the snarky comments, and the way her sister pushed her out.

"You've always overlooked it, Zen," Victoria had said over the phone, her voice both understanding and firm. "But now you're seeing it for what it is—dysfunction, envy. Chia's always been jealous of you."

And Zenya had to admit it—she could no longer deny the truth. The dress, the family gatherings, the constant exclusion all built up to this moment. She was done pretending that everything was okay.

With a sigh, Zenya pushed herself harder on the run, telling herself that *this* was what was important: being real, being true to herself. Because in the end, the dress, the wedding, the family gathering's —they weren't about the perfect picture. They were about authenticity. And Zenya was ready to reclaim that, even if it meant stepping away from the people who'd never truly embraced her.

CHAPTER 17

WEDDING BLISS

Triangles deserve no attention. The curtain has been pulled open, and the bright light shines. Big sister Chia has been changing the truth for over a decade. She gossiped about her younger brother, Cash, continuously sending information to *Asian E-News* in hopes of tarnishing his reputation. She even went as far as sending him a dead Giant Asian Hornet in an envelope through the mail. This huge insect has venom that can melt flesh. Chia has always been rotten. She spreads false accusations about her whole family and the DeRossi's.

For as long as Zenya can remember, it was always a triangle between her, Chia, and Aurora. On many occasions, Aurora lashed out and left abruptly from dinner tables and venues all around Asia. Yuan was never happy about her immature ways. The sisters agreed most of the time that Aurora started it, as they sat back, scratching their heads, not knowing what they had done to deserve this kind of behavior from their mother. Aurora was regarded as banausic and showed a lack of empathy during serious conversations, often saying, "Well, you know, your sister told people you are not a family person." Aurora's words. When brought to Chia's attention, she would play dumb, saying she never said that. Zenya just gave up trying to figure out which person was telling a lie or the truth, living her life without looking back, until she noticed that the systemic bullying was impacting her sibling's children. The family conflict needed to end with the first generation, Zenya had hoped.

Transcendence was a hot topic at the Buddhist monastery, as they believed that one must go through pain and suffering. It is detachment, a Zen-type of psychotherapy. Like the lotus that goes through the negativity of the dirt, the toxicity of the air tries to push it back down. Toxic relationships, on any level, are doing just that. They are playing a game, pushing us down. Cash always says, "You do not feed the beast. Laugh about it." Taped to Zenya's mirror are the words: "Don't fan the flames of their raging fire! Non-reaction is your best choice."

During a visit with a sixth-generation psychic, she expressed that Chia has purposely and permanently phased her out. She would send photos of her children to others in the family, but never to Zenya. She stated that Aurora was weeping in a blue room with blue hydrangeas. How in the world could a psychic know this?

When Zenya visited Aurora in Dubai, she recalled the flowered hydrangea sheets on the bed. As the words left Sierra's mouth, Zenya grasped the coincidence while tears welled up in the corners of her eyes, and Zenya let them stream down her cheeks. "You have felt irrelevant while striving to have a relationship with your siblings, and you are an overgenerous aunt. It is the parents that have perpetually made this extra challenging. They will reconsider when they need help. They do not understand solid personal beliefs. Chia knew this was the only way she could win," said Sierra. Zenya's revelation that Chia excluded her from specific events and the foundation's press briefing was clear.

The year's passing marked a change in the weather and set a new standard for the surrounding area. Auntie Zenya received a hand-delivered save-the-date card at her Hong Kong harborfront home. It was plenty of time to plan a perfect engagement party for her niece, as she received it during the summer solstice of the year prior. The date would be on the Chinese New Year of 2024.

Chia's oldest daughter, Sukhi, was finally taking the plunge into matrimony. It would be a winter wedding high up in the sky, a grand soirée with their closest friends and family to witness the nuptials. The celebration would occur at the Ritz-Carlton Sky 100th floor, with the spectacular light illuminating the Hong Kong skyline as a backdrop.

Executive Pastry Chef Marco would bring the wedding vision to life with the utmost attention to the wedding cake. Post-honeymoon, the newlyweds would whisper away on Zenya's private jet for an unforgettable four-week safari at the Serengeti's Four Seasons Lodge. Wedding present from all the aunts and uncles.

It was Saturday, February 10, and the Zhang Dynasty came together for a wedding, a delight to many, bringing rapid changes in the world around them. Everyone had taken their seats, and Zenya's friend John McAdams took center stage. Where did this guy come from? His confidence level was through the roof, and he hadn't ever picked up a microphone before in his life. He was towering over the crowd at 6'6", shouting out, "Drinks on me," as he commanded attention from the smoke-filled room.

With those dazzling blue eyes, it was hard not to stare at him. He looked dapper than ever in an Italian-tailored dark silk suit, Gucci loafers, black sunglasses, and an $88,000 Patek Philippe chocolate-brown alligator strap watch with 18k yellow gold. He stood on stage, smiling down at Zenya, towering over a room of 600 guests.

"Cheers!" the crowd clapped, whistling, shouting back, "Woowooahhh." McAdams, picking up the handheld mic, shouts back, "No, people, let me finish my sentence. Cheers is my softball team. How many fingers?" He holds his thumb up to the crowd. Smiling down at Zenya, he says, "And what do you do for a living, you sexy thing?" as he thought to himself, *I know what this pretty little thing will be doing later tonight.* Reserved, Zenya was embarrassed and yelled back, "I am a modern-day Queen," because saying "Ice Princess of the Zhang Dynasty" or "hedge fund broker" would be all too funny.

Never losing his punchline, "Well, baby, I'm an 1888 king, and I think we just found my future queen of Prussia. We will have a daughter named Abigail to tell this story to someday," said McAdams. The crowd's sound effects were a combination of clapping, cheering, and laughing. "Well, look at all my 'laughaholics' out there," said McAdams.

One more hour of comedic jokes, and he took his head out of the clouds, returning to earth as he approached Zenya's table. "See, I told you I'm hilarious," said McAdams. Zen winked up at him, realizing he had been drunk or high since the day they met. "Your parents are still annoyed with you. They told the Pilot boy that they need to book a cruise to spend time with you, but they do not want to be with the GP. Now look at who has adopted my language—'general public.' You hated that word," he thought as he kissed her forehead. "It's called savvy sailor nowadays, kid. Get ready for round two, my queen," said McAdams.

"Who would ever think you would end up in stand-up comedy? Hedge fund guru to comedy," said Zenya.

Vickie was looking down at her watch. There was no way she wanted to be hungover for the shareholder's meeting tomorrow. She knew when it was time to call it a night. "Thanks again for the invite, McAdams. It was nice meeting you, Sherrie," Zenya extended her hand. "I hope you two make it to the Swiss Alps. Just remember, the Chalet Restaurant is only open in Winter, and that truffled fondue is to die for."

The smartass had to chime in, saying, "I recall the Landermatt hotel's wine cellar contains a stellar private collection of Château Mouton-Rothschild labels, don't you remember that Zen?" asked McAdams. "What is the name of your hotel again? It is in Vail, right?" Kicking her foot under the table at McAdams, thinking this uneducated bimbo could barely say a sentence without slurring her words.

"The Chedi Landermatt, the Swiss Alps, which is in Switzerland," said Zenya as she winked back at McAdams. "Check it out sometime. However, one must be 21 to get into the bars."

"Touché, Zenya," said McAdams as he rubbed his foot on the back of her ankle.

She stood up and leaned over just far enough so that McAdams could catch a glimpse of her cleavage, kissing him on his forehead. His cheeks turned red. He was blushing with the excitement of his hard-on. Ah, yes, she still has it going on, the one that got away, he thought to himself.

"Again, it was a pleasure meeting you. Sherrie, take care of this handsome man as he is very special to me," said Zenya, who spent the last hour mingling with family and friends.

The hot topic was Carlos, and her comment was no comment. She preferred not to speak about Victoria's dad. It was sad enough, the thought of his passing, and that her best friend Victoria couldn't make it to her niece's special day.

The wedding was a success. Zenya was delighted that McAdams was able to make it. As she was leaving the ballroom,

Cash grabbed her hand. "I barely saw you all night. Where have you been hiding?"

"Well, you know, mingling," said Zenya.

"That was quite a show McAdams put on. That boy is still in love with you—give him a second chance? Have you talked to Victoria about him yet?" said Cash. Cash doesn't think either of the McAdam brothers, John or Conor, are good for Zenya or Victoria, but he really has been putting effort into the friendship with you throughout the years. Maybe... maybe he's not so bad after all, said Cash.

"We are grownups now. This is not college. And besides, he has Sherrie now to play head games with," said Zenya.

"That chick is hot. What is she, 21 or 18 years old? Confess?" asked Cash.

Rolling her eyes, she just nodded as he shrugged his muscular shoulders.

Cash escorted Zenya outside to meet her driver, Juan, saying, "Get home safe, love you, sis, and when my son gets married to Mohammed one day, I know that he will call upon your event planning expertise," said Cash as he squeezed her right shoulder as she sat down on the black Beluga leather of her Kingfisher blue Bentley Mulsanne.

"I love you too. We will leave for New York right after the board meeting. Please don't be late, Cash," said Zenya.

"You are a beautiful soul, Zenya, and empathetic of everyone. Why don't you have kids already?" said Cash.

"You sound like Aurora," said Zenya.

Cash chuckled as he walked away from the car. He thought this was the tipping point between his two sisters. The end at which a series of small changes or incidents becomes significant enough to cause a more considerable, more meaningful change. He couldn't quite put his finger on it, but he knew something was wrong. They were different, but leaving Zenya out of the wedding plans was not right, he thought. And Zenya was such a good sister, never calling Chia out on her odd behavior. It just never made any sense to him. As if Jasmine and Sukhi might have enjoyed Zenya's company better than their mother.

CHAPTER 18

MCADAMS

Waking up to her alarm at 5 a.m., she pushed snooze and rolled back over, placing her pillow over her throbbing head. She glanced over to see McAdams in her bed. "Why? Why are you in my bed? We said this would never happen again," Zenya said, holding her forehead.

"Well, it happened again, my little princess," John replied as he kissed her on the forehead.

She was not okay. It was like a turtle crawling back into its shell—hiding and also upset that she had let her guard down again with him. It was the truth. She had always had a massive crush on him ever since the day they met, when she was twelve years old. They sat by the Hampton beach campfire, and he handed her a sweater. She knew then he was her guy.

It's just that every time she lets her guard down with him, he breaks her heart all over again. When will this ever end, she thought? She would then ignore him, and he'd come crawling back time and time again, like a little lost dog.

They had another bout of wild morning sex, prompted by lots of thrusting and hair-pulling—followed by a hot steamy shower with another go-round.

McAdams was distracted, watching the Shanghai-Hong Kong Stock channel while percolating coffee and heating two chocolate croissants in the oven. He yelled, "Can't believe you still have this percolator!"

As McAdams patiently waited for his perc, as he called it, while reading what's new in *The Wall Street Journal*, Zenya walked from the bathroom naked, wrapping her hair in the white Egyptian cotton towel. Not responding, she studied the humming lovebirds inside the atrium Zen Garden, reminiscing about the coldest day in the Hamptons when they sat around that bonfire.

He slowly kissed the back of her neck as he set down the freshly brewed coffee on the quartz table in her bedroom. "What are we doing today?" he asked.

"You know I have to get to the office. Big meeting this morning with the shareholders," Zenya replied.

"Who will take over now that Carlos is gone? Do you think Victoria will keep the title?" McAdams asked.

"I would imagine so," Zenya said.

"I've missed you, Zenya. Can't we try to make this work again? It's sad enough with your brother's passing, and now Carlos. I know he was always like an uncle to you. Two deaths, and now a wedding. You see, life is short," McAdams said softly.

She pushed his hand away as she leaned down to pick up the coffee mug. "I have to get dressed. This was fun, but you must go now. Would you mind giving Sherrie a big hug from me? I still can't imagine how you ditched her last night. That was rotten," Zenya said, her voice tinged with frustration.

He looked disappointed, avoiding her gaze. "When you left the Ritz, I realized it wasn't over," he said quietly.

Zenya zipped up her Chanel skirt, a sudden knot tightening in her chest. "My driver brought us back to the Four Seasons. Sherrie gathered her things and headed to the Hong Kong airport to catch the first flight out to California. My driver drove me here. Sherrie is a big girl. We've only been on a few dates. It's not anything serious," McAdams explained, his voice soft but determined.

Zenya was left speechless, her heart racing. His words hit harder than she expected. Her poker face faltered for a moment, her breath shallow. Grabbing her keys from the foyer coffee table, she turned to face him.

"Don't forget to lock up, John. We'll continue this conversation on the plane to New York, where you can't run off and escape from me. I'll have your full attention for 16 hours," Zenya said, her voice steady but challenging.

"That is, if you still want me on your fancy G5. Sure, twist my arm. But don't invoice me $350K for this charter," John teased, the edge of humor not quite masking the tension between them.

"You're funny. Eight of us are headed back on that plane, and my calculations add up to $43,750," Zenya replied with a wry smile. Always knowing Zenya was brighter than him, John thought to himself that the energy spent on education is never wasted. Still, in business, the goal was to hold onto cash, even if the pressures were mounting.

The team meeting took over the conversation as they boarded the plane. Steve Toosa dominated the discussion. "Understand cycles are much more than revenue passenger miles. In the short term, we'll face some pressure due to the downtime at JP Morgan. Steve, in early March, that slide mentioned growing from the $3 billion research—are they still legit, or are you withdrawing that?" John asked, leaning forward.

"In the short term, the balance sheet has taken a hit, given the uncertainty of it all. We're not going any further than that. Today, we'll focus on getting stronger with higher cash flow growth," Zenya answered confidently.

John nodded. "Anything else you can do to make the balance sheet better?"

"We'll continue to stay positive and reduce aftermarket requirements. We've been hit hard, but we won't take the defeatist view. We'll control our destiny and the company's long-term projection," Zenya said firmly.

"Meeting adjourned," Zenya concluded. "Cash, we need to split. It's time to head to the plane. I'm dreading Carlos's celebration of life party—if the funeral wasn't bad enough, but we must be present to support Victoria."

"Let me guess—John is flying with us?" Cash asked, raising an eyebrow.

"You're psychic. How did you know?" Zenya laughed.

"He already texted me that he's bringing the bubbly, you slutty sister of mine. Yo, Jellybean, remember what Dad would say about playing with boys," Cash teased.

"Come on, please don't make me feel worse than I already do. McAdams may be a lost puppy, but for today, he's my lost puppy," Zenya said, rolling her eyes.

"Yesterday's history today is still a mystery, and tomorrow is an opportunity," Cash replied.

"I remember. I loved when Dad would tell us that," Zenya said, her voice softening as the memories of her father lingered in the air.

"Did you know that Victoria was handed an envelope at the funeral with her name typed on it? It was from her father's best friend, Attorney Giraldo. She waited all this time to open it. Inside, the note read, 'Victoria, your father was one hell of a gentleman, and he loved you more than life itself.' The envelope was inside Carlos's biometric safe deposit box in the Caymans," Zenya explained, her voice catching slightly.

"She'll be stronger now. But it does suck, his passing so suddenly," Cash said, his tone somber.

"Zenya, she's lucky to have you," John said quietly, his voice softer than usual.

"What did the note from her father say?" Steve Toosa asked, leaning forward.

"Something to the effect that the market could be very lucrative—significantly investing in A.I., electric vehicles, and battery charging stations. I think it's an intelligent move to add NIO to our portfolio. Carlos felt it would only be for those who take advantage of it early on," Zenya explained.

As she spoke, Zenya's mind was elsewhere, her thoughts scattered between the weight of her brother's death, the mystery of Carlos's last words, and the nagging pull of McAdams, who seemed to be walking a fine line between sincerity and distance. Could he really be the one? Or was he just another fleeting moment in her turbulent life?

Just as Zenya reached for her phone, she felt a familiar presence beside her. McAdams stood there, watching her, his eyes searching for hers.

"Zenya," he said, his voice low. "What if… What if I told you I was ready to take a leap? No more running away."

She froze, the words hanging in the air. Was this the moment? Would this time be different? Or would she find herself alone again, heartbroken and uncertain?

The plane's door closed with a soft thud, and Zenya had to make a choice.

CHAPTER 19

DISCOVERY

"Mom is sober, rightfully attending AA three times a week and shockingly volunteering at the local homeless shelter," said Chia. "That is impressive," said Zenya.

"Aurora and I talked yesterday," Chia said gently. "She's been in denial, insisting she never had a drinking problem. But now, she says this change in her life is her way of trying to make peace with the family. It seems like sweating and helping others has really touched something in her heart

"Please stop with your bullshit lies. Let me correct myself: Cash and I continue to have questions about the countless times mother would leave abruptly. How about, for starters, last Christmas Eve on Cash's yacht when she flew back on the helicopter? Or your daughter's birthday party, when she proudly stood up stating that she was abducted by aliens? How about when she said you have no ambition and live off your inheritance?" said Zenya.

"Keep going. Can't you give her a pass? She is trying this time," said Chia.

"Keep going, no problem, I can do this all day. How about grams' funeral in the middle of that classic eulogy? This crazy lady swore she was adopted. When she pulled out of your driveway, crashing into your housekeeper's car? Remember that episode when she drank a bottle of wine standing up, declaring that her children and grandkids meant nothing to her because we give her cheap gifts? The ribbon-cutting at the Xian Gallery, when she claimed to be tired from traveling, yet it was the combination of mixing antidepressants with vodka. Should I continue, Chia? McAdams just walked in, and I must say goodbye for now. I can no longer watch your inconsistency. All you do is play on both sides. You are a hypocrite, and you will never change. When one sibling was arguing with mom, you would run to cozy up to her, gossiping about all of us. You will never change, and I don't trust you or your motives," said Zenya.

All she heard on the other end was dead air as Chia hung up

the phone without a rebuttal. She couldn't acknowledge her sister was right once again.

"John, is that you? "I am out back," said Zenya. Kissing her forehead, he went to grab the open bottle of champagne. Coming back, he leaned down to kiss the back of Zenya's neck. "Let me guess, that was Chia," said McAdams. "You can tell by my tone or my red cheeks," said Zenya. "You can try, and try, and she will never like you no matter what you do. COVID-24 days or not," said McAdams. As he topped off her glass with bubbly, he reached into his side pocket, taking out a blue box.

It was that distinctive Tiffany blue box that every girl wanted to see. As he got down on one knee, he said, "Open, princess." Her eyes watered. *What is this man doing?* she thought. She slowly untied the white ribbon, opening the box. Her heart was beating faster and faster. It was a blue diamond of 2.51 carats bordered with diamonds in a platinum setting. He took the ring out of the box, putting it onto her finger. Her hand was shaking. "Will you marry me, Zenya? I have loved you since the day I laid my eyes on you. Please marry me, say yes," said McAdams. As she kissed him, bending down to him, sitting on his lap now. "Yes, yes!" said Zenya, as she bit his earlobe ever so gently. She had a flashback, remembering this one-of-a-kind $10 million advertised ring in the Tiffany window when she was in New York visiting McAdams. Her birthday was in December, and he often called her Capri when she would get upset with him. They made love three times.

Now, out of breath, McAdams wiped his forehead, chuckling. "Not bad for a forty-year-old. You will be my sex slave—sugar mama now and forever, Mrs. Zenya," said McAdams. Zenya couldn't believe that he had finally taken the plunge. He was the only one she could see herself growing old with, laughing through the good and bad times. They were best friends. They fell asleep watching the full moon over the harbor.

McAdams had a meeting in his Hong Kong office the following day and then met his partner at Nasdaq for the closing bell. She had nothing scheduled until noon. Zenya was in Hong Kong and would have to wait for Victoria to wake up to share the engagement news. She sent Victoria a photo text of the Tiffany box.

It was officially 3 a.m. in North America, and she couldn't wait any longer to call Victoria.

Eight thousand forty-five miles away, and she had to share the news. Zenya called Victoria, and she answered on the first ring.

"Guess what?" said Zenya.

"You are pregnant?" said Victoria.

"No, guess again," said Zenya.

"You murdered Chia?" said Victoria.

"No, silly girl, think again," said Zenya.

"What? I don't know. I'm half asleep. It's 3 a.m. here. I can't guess. Please tell me right now," said Victoria.

Zenya snapped a photo of her ring and said, "Look at your phone."

Hearing screams,"OH MY GOD, when—wait a minute—McAdams proposed to you?" said Victoria.

"Yes, he did, my friend," said Zenya, as tears started rolling down her face, and her mascara was running. "And of course, you said yes. All those times you broke it off with him to end up right here, I knew it. He has always been your soulmate. You have always been his number one. When is the special day, you lovebirds?" said Victoria. "No date, nothing is planned yet, not even the engagement party. It just happened," said Zenya.

"It took COVID to wake him up. He finally stopped taking you for granted. Life is short, and we have all learned that. Walking around, scared to breathe on anyone, wearing masks... It was just a matter of time that McAdams would cave in. He met his match with you, and we have all said that for years. Even Cash loves him," said Victoria.

"I know, but remember Sherrie, he brought her to my niece's wedding?" said Zenya.

"Oh please, Zen, that made you jealous, and he still ditched her, waking up the next morning in your bed. Congratulations, I will have champagne at Happy Hour today, and I am going back to bed now. I love you both," said Victoria. Victoria hung up, calling Victor.

Rays of the sunrise shined into the bedroom. McAdams entered the bedroom, drawing open the curtains, greeting her with green juice.

"Good morning, wifey. What time is dinner?" said McAdams. "Dinner? Make reservations, wifey no cook. I have a 4pm appointment at the museum. We will be making plans for the anniversary dinner," said Zenya.

"I will prepare a perfect bath for you. See you at 5 p.m. at the Ritz. I love you and enjoy your afternoon with your family. Play nice with Chia and mommy dearest Aurora," said McAdams. "Play nice with your Wall Street tribes," said Zenya.

Admiring her sparkling ring, she untied her robe, dropping it to the floor as she placed one leg into the copper bathtub. Peacefully relaxing, wondering just how blissful her life was, she started reminiscing. She worked hard, and it was now time to start meditating on a new chapter in her life, she thought. Tired of the whispers behind her back that she had no children yet, Miss Perfect, some even would say, or that her newest watch was not that nice. The one constant in her life was that she continued to have the same recurring dreams of tsunamis and Xi'an terracotta soldiers dressed in ancient armor.

Closing her eyes, she thought about how real her dream felt—the visualization of a terrible tsunami on its way from the Canary Islands. The whole east coast of the United States had no warning. They had no sign. Running as fast as she could, hand in hand with her love, they reached a dune with trees. Climbing up the Japanese plum tree, she was hanging upside down like a monkey holding on for dear life. The waves were enormous. She had to close her eyes and pray. Her love was there on the other tree branch, also holding on for dear life. She must have chosen the weaker tree branch, as it was starting to sway back and forth, a crack slowly and now snapping in half. The tidal wave washed in, taking nearly everything in sight back out to sea with it. It was their only chance to run to the mountains, she thought.

Running again for dear life, out of breath and dripping with sweat, she could hear voices screaming, sorrow everywhere, people weeping. They made it just beyond the tennis courts, then passed the employee parking lot where she saw two Xi'an soldiers. They looked as if they were frozen in time, almost robotic with a bronze coating. With a deep voice in Chinese, they simultaneously said, 你在跑向哪裡？ (*Where are you running?*)

Stopping to look back, she said, "I promise we will be right back after this wave returns out to sea."

As if they were in some camp or shelter area and were not supposed to leave those quarters, they were running again as fast as they could, passing the RV vans, tour buses, making their way up a stainless-steel ladder to only reach the top of the building. She looked around, noticing that it was the rooftop of the high-rise building where she currently resided. How could this be, as if she was running in circles, never reaching beyond her home? Looking down from the 21-story concrete building, she noticed a flexible thin screen that almost resembled a trampoline.

In the run for dear life, she lost her loved one and couldn't see where he ran to get out of harm's way from the wave, surely to wipe out their beach community. As she looked back, she was face to face with the 120-foot tidal wave, and she awoke, out of breath, gasping for air.

As a young child, she often daydreamed, thinking about the dreams she had been having. For as long as she could remember, she had been writing them all down in a dream logbook and would spend hours analyzing and picking apart each item of the dream, deciphering what that symbol meant, meditating deeply on the color of each item and how she felt in the dream. Zenya knew that the "Terra Cotta Warriors and Horses" were sculptures made from terracotta. She represented both the army of Qin Shi Huang and the first Emperor of China. Never showing evidence of learning this in school, she often wondered why the recurring dream about an emperor from 210-209 BC. Was it something she experienced in a past life, or a warning of what was to come?

Although some local farmers discovered figures dating back to the 3rd century BC in 1974 in Xi'an, perhaps it was time to put a call into Allen Cyers for that psychic reading he had promised her.

She thought maybe she was one of those 8,000 soldiers in a past lifetime. Just what did it all mean? She made her way out of the tub, drying off her suntanned, lean body and lathering natural lavender lotion on her voluptuous frame. Coconut oil in her hair as she walked out to her balcony door to overlook the harbor. She called McAdams to express how happy he had made her. A moment later, Victoria was calling John.

Later, Zenya said, "I love you so much!" He clicked over to hear screams in his ear.

"Congratulations, I approve, and I am coming to see you both," said Victoria.

"Of course, you are besties for life. Zenya misses you. Will it be a surprise? We have dinner reservations at the Ritz," said McAdams.
"Yes, I will arrive around 9 p.m. and will make the rest of the arrangements," said Victoria.

They chatted about the market for a few more minutes, but Zenya's mind was racing. She hung up the phone abruptly, her pulse quickening. Without hesitation, she dialed Victor.

"Forget the flight plans," she snapped. "We're taking the underground tunnel. It's faster, more discreet. Meet me there if you want, but I'm going."

The words hung in the air, a challenge, a mystery. What was she really planning?

The following weekend, Victoria and Zenya flew back to the States. They were instructed not to drink any booze, no vitamins, no RX drugs, and to only eat clean. Monday morning, they had an appointment at Dr. Yates's office in Manhattan to freeze their eggs. The cost to store your eggs in liquid nitrogen runs USD 60,000.00. It will be for a 10-year package with a choice to move their eggs off-site to long-term storage at the Svalbard Global Seed Vault for a reduced cost.

CHAPTER 20

TO THOSE WHO COME & GO

It was the museum's 100th anniversary, and the time had come to meet the shareholders and plan the annual gala dinner. Now was the time to post the family itineraries for the upcoming private jet trips.

"Chia told me that you could sit at the friends' table and not with the family. If you have a problem with that, she said you don't even need to attend," said Aurora.

"How dare her! I have just as many — if not triple — shares in this museum!" said Zenya.

As a child, Zenya often had recurring dreams of Xi'an Warriors. "Chia acts like a losing warrior. She's not going to push me out of my rite of passage. I belong at this table, at this event, and she needs to be an example to her children," Zenya declared.

"Are you dating McAdams again? She asked if you would be bringing him," said Aurora.

"Mom, listen, with all due respect, I'm asking you to saty out of this," said Zenya.

"Well, now that I'm sober, I'm trying to be in my daughters' lives as much as I can," said Aurora.

"I hear you, but you should have made peace with your mother. You treated her horribly, and you know it. Garnet didn't deserve that from you. She was the monarch of this family, and Cash and I miss her dearly," said Zenya.

"Chia shows her feelings. She doesn't believe anyone should live past 75," said Aurora.

"She what? What are you talking about?" asked Aurora.

"Senicide—you know, the last chapter of life. It's about aging and death, like in folklore. She's always been that gypsy-witch type," said Zenya.

"I don't understand any of that. All I know is she often plays with angel cards, and I don't like it," said Aurora.

"Mom, they say that great civilizations aren't brutally murdered. They say they commit suicide. Haven't you ever heard of Arnold Toynbee? He wrote about the rise and fall of civilizations, 26 societies," said Zenya.

"Why are you such a black-and-white daughter? You never see any gray shade in anything, Zenya. You take after your father in that way. Now that we're dealing with COVID-24 and the 1.15 million worldwide deaths, let's not talk about this sad topic," said Aurora.

"It's like senicide, and whether you want to believe it or not, it all started in the New York nursing homes. How a Governor could send sick patients to nursing homes still baffles me. Something like 6,300 COVID patients spread that disease to our elderly," said Zenya.

"Daughter, how is McAdams? What has he bought you lately?" asked Aurora.

"Why deflect? You change the subject when you don't want to listen. Look back at the H1N1 pandemic. We know it lasted about 19 months, and they say 575,400 deaths worldwide. Today, most people recover from H1N1 swine flu, usually within a week. Mauricio showed me the reports that the hospitals were coding everything to COVID-24. Sadly, the world continues to go through this without a cure. It sure is a money-making billing scheme for the hospitals," said Zenya.

"No, I don't believe that and cannot agree with you, although I know we have stock in 3M. Listen, I called you to discuss seating charts. How did we end up discussing COVID?" said Aurora.

"No, you called to throw flames on the fire. My team has always coordinated the planning of the Zhang family events. Is there a problem with me continuing this? What now?" said Zenya.

"Your sister thinks you don't have time to continue planning these events. I recall when she thought you had too much time on your hands and sat at home, looking at fancy new appliances while polishing your nails all day," said Aurora.

"Mother, as you said, I work too hard and juggle too many things to stop working and find a nice husband. It's a shame I have all these skills and not one job," said Zenya.

"Thanks for your honesty," said Aurora.

"It's not honesty. Maybe now that you're sober, you'll learn that you should keep negative comments to yourself. Continue to be that humanitarian the world needs and stay out of my battles. You don't ever interfere with Cash's life. Please, I beg of you, do the same with mine," said Zenya.

"Agreed. Now, where should I tell your sister you'll be sitting?" asked Aurora.

"Mother, can you ever stick up for me? Learn to stay out of your children and grandkids' issues. I truly beg of you. You've caused enough conflict for a lifetime. One more argument, and I'll disown all of you. And I mean it. Just ask Garnet—she agrees with me. I have another call," said Zenya.

"Good. I didn't want to talk to you either. Goodbye, brat," said Aurora.

Xi'an, the Warrior, had saved Zenya once before from a mega-tsunami. He most certainly could save her from Chia. She was only seven when he first showed her mental telepathy through a dream. Transferring his thoughts to her mind had traditionally occupied the realms of either science fiction or the paranormal—she'd never told anyone.

Upon awakening, Zenya realized that no one had built five-star luxury resorts in outer space, including landing pads with full-service bars and Michelin restaurants. That sparked a business idea: *What if a billionaire commercial real estate developer teams up with the perfect family to guarantee a lifetime of endless infinity?*

Zenya had never forgotten about Xi'an. She still searched for him in her dreams as an adult, thinking of it as a kind of neurological Morse code between her and her warrior hero.

The annual gala dinner brought in people from around the world. Most Zhang parties were known to move mountains. With all the corruption in the world, it was an excellent time to let the guard down among friends. Zenya always knew who the backstabbers were in her family and with her friends. She would tell one family member one secret and watch how far it went, always with many twists and turns. She once heard that Chia was trying to seduce McAdams.

The drama and lies never ended. Zenya often confided in Garnet and knew that she might not have always played fair with her siblings, but she always had her grandchildren's best interest at heart—whether they knew it or not.

Zenya ended her day with a hike up on Devils Peak. She thought she had seen Amida, but it couldn't have been him. Or could it have?

CHAPTER 21

REINCARNATION

An hour before each shareholders' meeting, Carlos would receive a reading from the well-known Sara Abrams, a sixth-generation psychic.

"Good morning, Cathy," said Victoria as she placed her new Hermès Blue Crocodile Skin Leather Palladium Satchel on her desk.

"Hello, Victoria. I can't even believe you're here," said Cathy.

"It's business as usual. Please, let's not freak out today. Of all people, I need my father's assistant to remain calm," said Victoria.

"Understood. Nice Birkin. Your 9 a.m. is in the conference room. What time would you like Kipriani's delivered?" asked Cathy.

Victoria ignored her as she stepped out of the glass elevator, and her security guard, James Landers, opened the frosted glass door on the 14th floor.

Boasting views of Park Avenue, the 1,000-square-foot office overlooked the balcony atrium, where there was a full-service bar, only serving the finest and freshest ingredients, light caviar, and other assortments of snacks. The conference table was an oval cherry wood table, surrounded by twenty black chairs. The walls had cherry wood panels. Two 70" smart televisions adorned each end of the room. Most employees of

Carlos would be found outside, taking a break on the oversized balcony, reading the WSJ on a sunny day.

The telephone on the table rang.

"Victoria DeRossi, can I help you?" said Victoria.

"Hello," came a soft-spoken, muffled voice. Victoria could not believe her ears.

"Ciao, daughter, how are you doing? *Tutto bene*? It would help if you had a nice glass of Brunello with that orecchiette and broccoli rabe, overlooking the Viareggio harbor and the breathtaking Versilian coastline, instead of being at work," said Carlos.

"Dad, is that you? Who is this?" said Victoria.

"It would help if you were in Italy. It's the only place you truly relax. How is Cathy? Give her my regards. Tell her I miss that strong cup of espresso and that tight ass," said Carlos.

One minor technicality—Carlos had been dead for only a day.

Victoria, nearly fainting and out of breath, was speechless. She had many questions for her father: How old is God? What does heaven scent smell like? Is there a mandatory dress code, or are you all naked? Have you been reunited with your loved ones, and are Santiago and Sofia young or the same age as when they died? What about your loved ones from a previous life? Are they reborn as humans on earth or in space? Can you see into the future, and whom will I marry? What resort and stocks should I invest in next? Would you have changed anything while on earth, or are you still on planet earth, floating on some celestial level? Why is the sky blue?

Swaying to the right, she leaned on the table. Diedre walked over to her and said, "It's all right. He's in a better place now." How did she even know it was Carlos? Yet again, why would she not know that? Victoria thought.

The words *Policía* flashed over the Boeing B-17 "Flying Fortress" picture on the wall. Victoria blinked and looked again at the frame. Was she hallucinating?

Calmly, Carlos said, "Girls, run, get out of there now."

Policía. Policía, flashing multiple times. Two police officers were on the ground, pointing rifles with red lasers into the conference room. Diedre was hiding in the corner behind the tree.

Victoria called for James as she hit the panic button under the table. The woman opened the atrium door, entering the room as James simultaneously ran in.

"Victoria. Come to me," said James.

"No, I'm not leaving Diedre here all alone. What is going on here?" said Victoria.

Eight FBI agents swarmed inside the building, ordering security to lock down the building. The essence of time was a real thing. A helicopter was at eye level in the room. Victoria could not believe what was happening. Were they being raided?

"We have a warrant to search the property, and you need to come into custody with us to answer a few questions about your father. He had been unknowingly funding money into the Italian mafia—or some call it laundering money—and no one knew. An old friend of your father's, named Mario DiCapone, originally owned that Fiji resort.

The Larsons had ratted him out. If all went well, they would have arrested Carlos, but he died before it could happen," said the agent.

Victoria remembered that her father had won that resort in a high-stakes gambling bet. She thought it was the Larsons. There was never any exchange of money.

Carlos had kept the black leather briefcase on the plane, which never left his sight. It must have been something important inside, because he kept singing *Fly Me to the Moon*. The Larsons also pretended that they had won the Fiji resort. I guess Mario DiCapone had always been the silent partner, after all.

Victoria was confused. In addition to the man's voice, it sounded just like her father. Now, this is impossible, she thought. She couldn't believe he was still alive... or dead.

Her head started pounding as her heart raced, feeling a sharp pain in her chest. She reached for her cell phone.

"Officers, I am pleading the Fifth Amendment and the right to remain silent. I wish to speak to an attorney," said Victoria, who knew she would have to call upon criminal defense attorney Vaughn Murphy.

CHAPTER 22

FRUITION

The healthcare crisis from 2020 hit an all-time high, with endless rules that made no sense. Staggered seating, six feet of distance, 50 percent of customer capacity, and extended closures of local restaurants, store chains, and mom-and-pop shops led to the collapse of the dollar. They were then lowered to 25% indoor seating capacity in Democratic liberal cities such as Los Angeles, CA, North Caldwell, NJ, Detroit, MI, Boston, MA, and even the global power, cosmopolitan New York City,

NY. The elite realized back in the '80s that this would take over 40 years to implement worldwide, officially.

They wanted their agenda grandfathered in, where the Jones III grandson would be heir to the New World Order club. If people just woke up one day to the New World Order, where would the fun be in that? This was the global elite's game of monopoly, and people who were not from the elite families—the third vaccine-free generations of family ties—made it more fun to sit, listen, play, and watch.

The breakdown of society was a game to them, and they enjoyed watching the general public suffer. The manufactured volcano eruptions, Brazil and California fires, tsunamis, earthquakes, tornadoes, and hurricanes were also part of the plan to relocate people. They wanted people, whom they called ants, all squeezed into cities, in big buildings with a minimum of twenty floors or more, in 500 sq. ft. apartments with no windows—just a wall with a sun and a moon that would turn on at the appropriate time of day. With this type of sardine-like building rising into the sky, they could roll out 5G, which would be Phase III of the new plans: renewable energy, solar power plants, E.V. vehicles, and charging stations. China took down the grid when another Republican president took over, and they knew it was now time for the ants to succumb to this clown in the White House. They had one shot or feared having to wait another four more years for the takeover.

People thought it was customary to ditch their cars to ride the speed bus, train, or even work in the same building where they lived. They fell into the belief that global warming was happening, and they had to give up certain luxuries to create a better world for their children's children and so on. No one believed that the end to emissions in 2025 was for real. Yet little did they know, the elite would take away all vehicles from the road. These elites had second and third homes in space—some even on different planets.

Debate with someone who insists that they will not succumb to the elite party taking away their cars. We all witnessed the president sign the executive orders to end the Keystone Pipeline and fossil fuels. The year we had no gasoline to start the cars anymore, people finally woke up. These elites had second and third homes in space, some even on different planets.

Eugenics, global warming, food shortages, and a one-world currency came to fruition just as predicted by the Felix Jones of the world. Those with 401(k) savings, stocks, and bonds nearly had a stroke when the market collapsed. Retirement savings were blown, for what? They scratched their heads, believing in their government: masks, hand sanitizer, and community shutdowns. Families were forced to live out their last days on

Earth in tiny, coffin-sized, Asian-style rooms. The 1% elite ruled the land and were the only ones permitted to roam freely.

That Reef Kevo knew what he was doing with the auto-shipment to homes. People lost touch with freedom when artificial intelligence took control that year, and it was nothing more than herding the people into a slaughterhouse. People became scared, lazy, and accepted the handouts of government money as they were convinced the vaccine would end the lockdowns.

The world was coerced into believing they would travel freely on an airplane without any vaccine documentation. They were squashing the dreams of young children from all around the world.

By 2024, national identification cards and thumbprints linked to cryptocurrency were the new norms, along with planet lockdowns. Central bankers could no longer keep the dollar system going. Terrorism, viruses, the world was now a scary place to live, and the government could play a significant role with the media to cause lockdowns. The government never protected those poor Americans. 2021 death tolls reached one million just a few years ago.

Anyone on Earth who died due to an unpredictable accident, organ failure, or a heart attack was coded as a coronavirus death for the hospitals to make $88,000. They were in cahoots with the pharmaceutical companies, and it was indeed a medical billing numbers game. It was a numbers game that only the globalists were aware of. The average general public type of guy or gal had no idea, and those who said they knew about the one-world government were named everything from Republicans, witches, and idiots to farm people, crazy fearmongers with endless stories about wild conspiracy theories. Even though we knew that the vaccine led to martial law, these people were not psychic. They didn't want to be chipped, didn't want weird factions such as future diagnoses of narcolepsy or GBS.

We recall the coin shortage at most retail outlets, and that was when you still had grocery stores and shopping malls. The last of the survivors had been vaccinated, yet now and then, someone would rat a neighbor out who hadn't been convinced to take the shot or else. The "or else" factor was no flying, no more adventures overseas with friends and family, and no work-related travel, as A.I. took the jobs away when they uploaded the cloud to all humans' brains throughout the world.

That was the year all citizens in America laid down and let the government take care of them. Every family in America received $8,888 stimulus checks, along with free iPhones for all. Immigrants at the detainee center were granted citizenship by agreeing to the hand microchip, as no one knew about the actual underground organ chipping. Those in jail received the vaccine before the elderly in nursing homes in New York because the elite had a plan for them at NASA. Yet the governor, at the time of the breakout, was the first to stick people with the plaque into nursing homes, giving them a place to stay, which only spread the virus to the elderly. It was to cut a chunk out of the Social Security payables.

Now, some say it was a plot against population control, while others debated that he just made a mistake and that the fame and fortune of his book deal went to his head. Man, the guy even received an Emmy for his so-called "masterful" COVID briefings. Those woke said it appeared to be a reenactment of Warren's American political satire hit movie *Wag the Dog* and *Krumins Show*. Similarly, both were a comedic psychological drama about people living under a Big Brother weather bubble, having an ordinary life unknowingly, all the while on a movie set filled with actors pretending life was beautiful.

When they took the rights away from people, the states went bankrupt, weakening America. Three billion in tree programs, climate incentive grants, the Trojan list went on. The United States now has a Green New Deal, a pill for each meal of the day. Democrats could not get the cat back in the box. Once they started down this road to socialism, they had no way to turn around. They were reaching the 40-year mark and needed to close in on the promised land. China refused to take accountability for the virus, just as they continued to decline our recyclables. You could not find glass bottles any longer.

Some conspiracy theorists say that with the timeline of things coming to fruition and this new president, whom some call a clone, this was the first red flag to the elites that the NWO had begun. It should have been no surprise to the ants—human cloning produces a genetic copy of an existing person. Carlos visited the Center for Genetics and Society, and despite his shareholder friends, he could not wrap his head around why. What's the point? He didn't want to live forever.

Gillean, the chairman, comes across as a slick slimeball, yet sincere. He chuckles at Carlos for not giving in to having his clone. The second was the manufactured plague that reached all countries. The third is the planned stock market crash, which was rumored to start with the next Devils Coin (DC), an alternative for crypto enthusiasts' worth buying, boasted digital gold investor Gillean. He vomits old school, yet he is all for supporting the New World Agenda.

No accountability, no arrests, just slaps on the wrists, but the 65-year-old Jewish-Italian woman arrested for not wearing a face mask at the bagel joint she frequented daily for the past 30 years? No reading of her rights. All those so-called insane survivalist preppers had bought them up in preparation for the food shortages. They were the last 20% left who had refused the vaccine, living off the land now out in rural areas. They had been living off freeze-dried food, seeds, solar ovens, and water filters for so long now that it was not strange to those folks.

Their only link to the outside world was through shortwave radios.

The food had GMOs, but the soil and water were tainted with coronavirus, a new variant that made the Americans much sicker than COVID-24. By the time COVID-24 was here, we were all doomed.

Catherine A. Pitts predicted it all, and she had it all mapped out, calling him the Global One.

A president was once quoted as saying that he does not read the newspapers. He waits for the signals on the TV. It could be something as simple as "Bigfoot found in Stonehenge" to signal that it was time for Phase I. No more farming—agriculture, all a thing of the past. A writer, *Healthy Is Not a Size; It's a Lifestyle; Living GMO-Free in the 21st Century*, wrote about it. Hell, I believe she even coined the name "GMO-disease," and readers called her out of touch with modern agriculture. It has been predicted time and time again about famine, polluted air, and water.

Average working-class citizens had their rights taken away from them when that China virus came to America. We knew the soldiers brought it over to spread biological warfare. War, military, and fighting combat are also things of the past. The new norm was space games. Whoever had the biggest, best-built ship was, and is, the winner, they said.

The three words "Beast from the East," a headline story printed on the cover of every newspaper and on social media, was the Phase II signal. That news article was about a second blizzard hitting Britain, which is how the elites communicated. No speaking, no texting—just words right under the general public's nose. The first signal about the beast was back in 2018, which signaled that they had a vaccine, and it was time to spread the coronavirus.

The elites would get together annually at a Z5 summit. Each held out a number representing the state or country they would purchase. Restaurants closed in major cities because it was their rule. The land was dirt cheap, and no one wanted to buy retail or restaurant property linked to the virus, as they said the germ would live on surfaces. They even went as far as saying that the virus went into the land. Perfect opportunity for the elite to place their bids, without even having to railroad the owner out. They gave up after the third or fourth lockdown. Many spent their savings adhering to the city governors to meet the "new germ-free" code of hand-sanitizer stations at every other table and plastic shields.

The owners of these buildings paid a high percentage on a mortgage for 20-30 years, only to be shut down and eventually fold. The big elite would come in and not even have to purchase the land. Like Chernobyl gas masks, the New World Order was about killing 80% of the general public, leaving only 20% to be slaves and cater to the elite 1%. The general public? Hell, they took up too many resources. It was no surprise that the second-largest landholder was Fred Furner, who also owned most news outlets.

SPACE EXPEDITIONS

As humanity discovered the true potential of interplanetary travel, the gaze of Earth's populace shifted from the stars to the crises unfolding on the ground. Between the ever-controversial elections and the escalating spread of COVID-24, the public's sense of wonder was increasingly overshadowed by turmoil. Meanwhile, churches remained locked down, and Roman priests, now on social media, preached that the third vaccine booster was the harbinger of humanity's extinction. GMO-free food and religious services had become luxuries, accessible only to the elite who could afford private priests, much like they once hired butlers, chefs, and personal trainers.

After decades of anticipation, Trojan Galactic was finally on the verge of launching its space tourism service, promising journeys to the very edge of space. But at a cost of $530,000 per person, only the ultra-wealthy would have the opportunity to leave Earth behind.

Carlos, a 61-year-old businessman, had signed up for this privilege back in 2005. For $250,000, he secured five minutes of zero gravity beyond Earth's atmosphere. Upon his passing, the ticket was passed to his daughter, Victoria. She, a child once mesmerized by the stars from her rooftop patio, would soon fulfill the dream her father had once held for her. At the age of eight, Carlos had told her she was a bright star, destined for the vastness of space. On his 50th birthday, Victoria had given him a gift that left him speechless, a star of her own, immortalized with a wooden plaque he proudly displayed in his office.

Now, it was her turn. Carlos had dreamed of building a celestial empire in his name—a chain of luxury resorts scattered across the solar system: on the Moon, Venus, and beyond. Each resort would feature a shuttle landing pad, an observatory, and an Earth-like floor complete with live-streamed views of their home planet and screenings of classic Earth cinema. A fitness center, barista, and juice bar named *24/7Carat* would cater to the elite guests. Carlos had also invested in *Vanera-1*, the first probe to journey toward Venus—an Earth-like planet, but more exotic, with unique landscapes.

Carlos' vision extended to ten luxury resorts located within well-known constellations: *Lynx-5, Auriga-7, Cassiopeia-9, Cygnus-18, Lacerta-11, Lyra-22, Vulpecula-19, Bootes-29, Perseus-8,* and *Corona Borealis-28*. If all went according to plan, Trojan

Galactic would become the first private company to take tourists into space, with over 600 tickets already sold, including to celebrities like Austin Giber and Fernando Capprumo.

Rival firms weren't far behind. *Yellow Origin*, founded by Geoffrey Pesos of Blazom, and *Space-TripleX*, spearheaded by Elon Muskato of Gesla, were also preparing to launch their own commercial space missions. Space-TripleX had even announced their first lunar passenger—a Japanese billionaire eager to orbit the Moon.

Unlike the Apollo astronauts who endured months of intense training, the space tourists of tomorrow would need only three days of preparation. Trojan Galactic claimed the training would be brief, but thorough enough for passengers to "understand the choreography" and maximize their experience.

Victoria, along with other founding members, was invited to visit Trojan Galactic's *Spaceport of the Americas* in New Mexico.

The off-the-grid terminal featured an exclusive cigar lounge, a restaurant, and an interactive walkway—all designed with floor-to-ceiling windows for an unobstructed view of the launches.

The space tourism industry was drawing attention from billionaires and Wall Street investors alike. In October 2019, Trojan Galactic became the first space flight company to list its shares on the stock market, igniting a surge in investment. Could 2020 be the year the promise of space tourism finally took off?

But there was a deeper agenda behind the pandemic than the public realized. Phil Bate's vision of eugenics, mass vaccinations, and the chipping of humanity wasn't just about controlling the population on Earth—it was about preparing humanity for life on other planets. The "hand chip" was designed not just to track citizens but to ensure they could safely return to Earth after their space adventures. The nanochips, implanted during vaccination, had the unique ability to ground the human body—literally preventing people from floating away into space.

Meanwhile, the public was told that the mass vaccinations were to protect humanity from the COVID-24 virus, which would become a major obstacle for any Mars-bound missions. The metal alloy in the chips would ensure that those chosen to leave Earth would be safe from the environmental hazards of space travel. The race to vaccinate wasn't about control—it was about survival.

Anti-vaccine activists, gaining influence through social media, were skeptical of the official narrative. A report from the Center for Countering Digital Hate revealed that anti-vaxxers' social media following had increased by at least eight million people since 2019, stoking the fires of dissent. Yet for many, the future lay beyond Earth.

NASA's successful landing of *Perseverance* on Mars was a landmark moment. Striking photographs from the descent-stage's camera, capturing the rover's first moments on Martian soil, marked a pivotal point in the history of space exploration. But for Victoria, these triumphs paled in comparison to the journey she was about to embark upon.

During her flight to space, Victoria met Cleo Shephard, an actress who shared her passion for creating a luxury resort on the Moon. "Fly me to the Moon, and let us play on Jupiter and Mars," Cleo joked. "In other words, I'm all in."

"Vincent, when did you secure your seat?" Victoria asked.

"My grandmother..." Vincent began, recounting a tragic story of her death during the 2018 Hurricane ETA. He described how the paramedics had tested her for COVID-24, even though she had died from complications unrelated to the virus. "The first test was worse," he said. "They shoved the swab up her nose so far it felt like they were poking her brain. Later, I found out it was all part of a larger plan—some conspiracy to control the population with mercury-laced cotton swabs."

Victoria listened quietly. "I'm grateful I never had children," she said. "At least I won't have to worry about what the future holds for them."

"Well," Vincent replied, "the truth is, she was too old to live alone and too old to travel to space. But as for me, I'm here now, and I will make him proud."

Later, they gathered at the bar with the rest of the crew, knowing they'd soon be embarking on a journey beyond the stars. Before turning in for the night, they drank a cocktail made from purified water, chelation therapy, and a vitamin B12 drip to prepare for the next day's mandatory COVID test. The regimen was rigorous, but the stakes were higher than ever. This was no longer just a flight into space—it was the next step in humanity's future.

CHAPTER 24

THE DEPOPULATION AGENDA

Billionaires around the world have long been pulling the strings to shrink the global population. What began with 7.8 billion people was now nearing 750 million—a carefully orchestrated plan. Their ultimate goal was a population under 500 million, a controlled balance with nature. Furner's sprawling cattle ranches had become a sanctuary for the world's most powerful, the elite 1%, while the rest of the world continued to dwindle, left to fend for themselves in a new era of surveillance.

Xian and Garnet, two of the few remaining insiders, feared the widespread dangers of cloning falling into the wrong hands. The general public, distracted by the relentless flow of media and technology, refused to challenge the growing abuse of power. The Singapore government's safety protocols were a perfect example: a centralized database, publicly accessible, tracked the movements of every citizen. It was a chilling violation of privacy masked as protection, one that could easily identify individuals through location data alone. While this might sound innocuous, it wasn't hard to see the potential for misuse.

Elsewhere, governments implemented increasingly invasive measures. In Poland, a mandatory selfie app required citizens to upload pictures every day during their 14-day isolation or face police visits. In Israel, phone tracking had been used to enforce quarantines, a program only stopped after public outcry. What troubled Garnet more than the protocols themselves was the involvement of the United Global Network, which had orchestrated many of these measures under the guise of public health.

Meanwhile, scientists remained baffled by the Antonine Plague of 165 AD, much like they had been by the origins of the COVID-24 outbreak. What was once thought to be an isolated pandemic had revealed itself to be part of a much larger scheme. By the time the virus spread globally, Kates & Co. had already turned to more sinister methods, using nano-dust sprayed in HAARPZ chemtrails to manipulate the soil, stripping crops of nutrients and altering human DNA through genetically modified foods. The truth? Buying and selling humans was never about profit; it was about control. One world denomination, governed by a select few, was the real aim.

When COVID-24 hit, the initial reports were simple. It didn't seem to affect those with O+ blood type. But the virus mutated, and the numbers the media reported began to spiral out of control. What had been seen as an opportunity to push a global vaccination agenda turned into a multi-faceted scheme, one that included testing, surveillance, and the eventual global control of population through selective, mass inoculations.

In truth, the initial outbreak wasn't nearly as deadly as reported, and the narrative around COVID-24 served a different purpose. While some fell victim to the virus, others experienced only mild symptoms, or none at all. Yet the media continued to peddle the message of a deadly pandemic, keeping people quarantined, restaurants closed, schools shuttered, and airports empty. It wasn't about protecting the people; it was about controlling them. Behind the scenes, a strange pattern was emerging: the elite were working on a virus, not to kill but to control. Those who refused the vaccine would be subject to harsher measures, or worse.

As the world grappled with the latest pandemic, the elite pressed forward with their agenda. The Black Death had long been a historical tragedy, but now, in a world increasingly defined by technology and surveillance, they were orchestrating pandemics of their own making. SARS, Ebola, malaria—all of these diseases were experiments, building blocks in their long-term plan to depopulate the Earth.

Dr. Arturo Baci, a key figure in these developments, had worked tirelessly on perfecting the viruses. The SARS trials, initially thought to be inconclusive, were simply another step in his plan to manipulate public hysteria. The real weapon wasn't the virus—it was the fear.

And fear, of course, led to control. That's what had happened during the coronavirus pandemic. A simple, common flu had been transformed into a global crisis. People were conditioned to live in fear, wearing masks even as they traveled alone in their cars. Public spaces had become places of isolation, the streets eerily empty, everyone locked in their homes.

By 2024, even food had become a luxury. Grass-fed beef, once a staple for many, was reserved only for the ultra-wealthy. The masses were left to consume whatever scraps remained. The government, in its infinite wisdom, implemented regulations that turned even the most basic sustenance into a commodity, tightly controlled by the elite.

The collapse of local economies, such as in Puerto Rico, served as a blueprint for what was to come. Fluoride was added to the water to dull the minds of the general population. Only the tourists at elite resorts could enjoy the luxury of beef; locals were forbidden. In a cruel twist of fate, the cattle industry was ordered to stop supplying the general public, consolidating power into the hands of a few.

It was no surprise, then, that depopulation remained the central tenet of foreign policy. When the U.S. allowed immigrants to cross the border without vaccines, it wasn't out of compassion. The immigrants were given bitcoins, enough to ensure they would vote in favor of whichever elite-backed party was in power. Everything, it seemed, was a transaction.

The organs of the deceased were harvested and sent to secret locations, where they would eventually be used to clone new bodies for the elite. The Bate Center in New York became the heart of this operation, its emergency helicopters were designed to extract vital organs before they could deteriorate. These bodies, meant to replace the aging elite, would soon be the future of human civilization.

As the world grappled with the ramifications of these conspiracies, Victoria, still unaware of the full scope of what had been happening, started to connect the dots. Rumors swirled that her late father, Carlos, had been cloned, his wealth and connections too significant for anyone to ignore. Could it be true?

But that wasn't the only secret Carlos had hidden. Victoria discovered that cloning was not just a medical breakthrough — it was part of a larger, more sinister plan. She learned that the Zhang family, the powerful elite who controlled vast swaths of land and wealth, had known about these experiments for decades. Victoria's father had been involved with them, perhaps unknowingly, or perhaps as part of a high-stakes gamble.

And in a conversation with her friend Zenya, Victoria realized just how deep the conspiracy ran. Zenya shared stories of her own family's ties to the Zhang dynasty, and the startling revelation that alien life had been interacting with humans for centuries. They had even begun to clone and integrate alien DNA, creating a hybrid race that would soon dominate Mars — and perhaps even Earth.

For Victoria, the truth was stranger than fiction. The world she had known, full of luxury resorts and space-age technology, was a façade, hiding the dark reality of a planet on the brink of extinction. The Zhang family had already begun preparations to move humanity off-planet. But the question remained: could Victoria, with all her father's legacy, survive the coming storm? Would she be able to uncover the truth before it was too late?

CHAPTER 25

CORONAVIRUS HELL - 2030

Silenced and all alone out on the barge, Victoria sat in the dim light of the night, reflecting on what once could have been with him. The stars above, twinkling like forgotten dreams, seemed to offer no answers. She wondered, *If, when, and where* they would ever reunite again in a world filled with chaos, conflict, confusion, and turmoil. Trust had become a luxury few could afford, and the notion of true love felt like a distant memory — one she could barely hold on to. In this fractured reality, only love seemed real.

The news of the new COVID-24 Deltano variant spread like wildfire, and young children were dying at an all-time high.

What had begun as a conspiracy to thin the herd—taking out the weak, the fragile elderly, those with diabetes—was now running amok. Women were infertile, men impotent, and the pharmaceutical giants continued to peddle their drugs. The vaccines caused heart palpitations, inflammation, and even increased rates of blindness—genetically modified vaccines made with blood from aborted human fetuses, horses, pigs, and shark cartilage. The ultimate goal had always been clear: cross-species, the human race with animals.

Scientists had first identified a human coronavirus in 1965, causing nothing more than a common cold. But as Dr. Yates had explained, the pandemic could signal a scientific paradigm shift, an opportunity for those in power to accelerate innovation. However, innovation came at a cost. The brain chip, which could save humanity, was not available to all, and the population had to be reduced to only fifty million for the reset to take effect. The case studies from the first SARS-CoV-2, originating in bats, had been the starting point for a future that no one could fully comprehend.

As COVID-24 took hold, those who had received the vaccine couldn't live without their booster shots—administered twice a year, forever. What had begun in Wuhan's open-air wet markets had evolved into a global nightmare. The real story, one hidden from the masses, was that those in power—politicians, the elite, the 1%—had long been complicit in the disaster. Wet markets selling banned species like cobras, wild boars, and raccoon dogs allowed viruses to mutate, jumping from animals to humans. But this, too, was part of the plan.

The year was 2030, and the world stood on the brink of extinction. The New World Order had been fully implemented, and depopulation was at the core of their agenda. Dominated by mixed planetary cultures and secret societies, Earth had become a battleground for control. The 1% had perfected the art of cloning, controlling DNA, even creating life on distant planets. Those who were pregnant on Earth gave birth only to have their children sent to Pluto, where they would grow up as a twin of the original Earth-bound person. It was a twisted version of reincarnation, only this time, it was the elite who controlled the cycle.

Amber Alerts—once signals of missing children—were now used to alert the wealthy aristocrats and the alien world that clone pods were ready. The so-called alien abductions of the 1980s? Just another method of harvesting clones.

But the truth about the vaccines was more chilling. The PEG additive in the Pfizer and Moderna vaccines was not only harmful but also part of a grander design to control the masses.

The public, oblivious to the real dangers, continued to follow the path laid out for them. The pharmaceutical companies had been killing the poor for decades, systematically eliminating those deemed unworthy.

As food prices soared in 2030, undernutrition became widespread. And amid the chaos, headlines blared about divorce proceedings, billion-dollar fortunes, and plane debris falling from the sky, blamed on chemtrails. All the while, the people remained unaware, numbed by the constant barrage of news, distracted by the lives of the elite.

Infinity, LLC, home to the secretive Geonomics Cloning Team, was based in Switzerland and led by Dr. Richard Slate III. The estate was guarded by towering gates and adorned with ominous statues, a fortress of power hidden in plain sight. The wealthy made daily trips to the estate, while the general public remained clueless about the dark experiments taking place behind the walls.

Elliott, Samuel, and Brando—famous musicians from the Bella Band—had been spotted at Infinity decades ago. Rumors circulated that they had been cloned after contracting HIV in the '70s, their immortality ensured by the elite's insidious cloning program. The truth was far darker than anyone realized.

Victoria stood up, her reflection in the water of the barge suddenly interrupted by a flicker of light on the horizon. Could it be? Was someone coming for her? Or was it simply the stars playing tricks on her weary mind?

Her heart raced. She had to know the truth. The journey wasn't over. Not yet. And just as she prepared to set her mind to finding the answers, the water beneath her began to ripple, as if something—or someone—was stirring.

As the ripples grew larger, a shadowy figure appeared in the distance, gliding toward her. Could it be him? Or was it a trap set by those who controlled everything? The wind carried a familiar scent, a memory, but it was fleeting. She had no time to think.

In the distance, a signal blinked—a coded message she could barely comprehend.

And then, the unthinkable happened.

CHAPTER 26

MYSTERIES OF THE ZHANG LEGACY

Zenya jolted awake, her heart pounding with excitement as the remnants of her dream clung to her like a second skin. She had seen it again—the stars, vast and endless, stretching out before her, beckoning her to the unknown. The stars had never felt so close, so real, and she could almost feel them waiting, just beyond her reach. But Victoria was already there, out there among the planets, ready to welcome her into the new frontier of humanity's future.

It was time.

Zenya's hands trembled as she pulled herself up from her bed, still floating in the dizzying sense of possibility. The dream—no, the *vision*—was clearer this time. She had seen Victoria, standing on the edge of a massive spaceship, a gleaming silver pod that seemed to hum with energy. The bright lights of a distant galaxy shimmered around her, her face illuminated with awe and determination. Victoria, so close, yet so far away, was living the dream they had spoken about for years. She was already stepping into the unknown—and Zenya was right behind her.

Her mind raced with the implications for what was happening. The Zhang Legacy wasn't just a story—it was *real.* The secrets they had all fought to uncover, the truths hidden deep within that they had all fought to uncover; the truths hidden deep within the Southampton estate; the mysterious Geonomics

Cloning team, Dr. Richard Slate III—everything was coming to a head. The world was on the brink of a new era.

Zenya felt the pull, not just to follow Victoria, but to be a part of something greater, something monumental. Infinity was no longer just a dream. The golden age of space tourism was here, and it wasn't just for the ultra-wealthy elite. It was for everyone, for the masses who had been dreaming of this moment for generations. The stars were no longer an unreachable fantasy — they were a new world, waiting for humanity to claim them.

She would be there. She had to be.

The Southampton estate, once a place of mystery and shadow, now held the key to their future. The secrets within its walls would unlock the way to a life beyond Earth, a life where the unthinkable could happen. No longer would humanity be chained to the crumbling planet below. Space was the next frontier, and Zenya was ready to take her place among the stars.

The dream, the vision—it was just the beginning. There was so much more to uncover. *So much more to do.* She knew she would join Victoria, that she would follow her friend into the vast unknown. Together, they would face the mysteries of the Zhang Legacy and discover what lay beyond the stars. This was the future, and Zenya was determined to be a part of it.

The world was changing, and the time to act was now. The Zhang Legacy trilogy was about to explode into the next chapter—*Infinity*. And for Zenya, the journey was just beginning.

Infinity was waiting.

Get ready for a mind-blowing ride that will take you far beyond the stars. The stakes are higher than ever, and the adventure is just beginning. The secrets of the Geonomics Cloning team, the enigma of Dr. Richard Slate III, and the untold story of space tourism are about to unfold in ways you won't believe.

Hold on tight, because Infinity is only the start. Prepare for the breathtaking discoveries, the shocking twists, and the unthinkable revelations that await in the next chapter of this thrilling saga. And as the countdown to the stars begins, you'll be left breathless, yearning for more.

Get ready for the future. Get ready for Infinity.

CHAPTER 27

SILENT SIGNALS

McAdams sat back in his bed, the glow of his phone illuminating his face as he scrolled through an article that had caught his attention. The headline read, *"The Future of Cloning: Florida at the Forefront of Genetic Innovation"*. He wasn't particularly one for reading scientific journals or long-winded articles, but something about this topic intrigued him. Florida, the Sunshine State, had long been a hub for all things innovative and experimental, and this article delved into the state's latest progress in the realm of cloning. He couldn't help but wonder about the ethical implications, the potential medical breakthroughs, and whether anyone could truly predict where this technology was headed.

The article highlighted Florida's expanding role in cloning research, specifically in the fields of regenerative medicine and therapeutic cloning. The idea of cloning organs and tissues for medical purposes, perhaps saving lives through stem cell research, seemed like something out of a futuristic world. McAdams found himself captivated by the advancements—an industry that not too long ago seemed like something relegated to the pages of science fiction was becoming a tangible reality. The thought of cloned organs saving lives was no longer a distant dream. But what really grabbed his attention was the mention of some of the most cutting-edge research taking place right in Florida, specifically in Broward County.

His thoughts wandered to Zenya. Zenya was involved in some of the most secretive, high-level research in Florida, and the mention of Broward County and its cloning initiatives immediately made him think of her. She had been a key player in the ongoing work surrounding genetic research, and her intellect and passion for the field were unmatched. He admired her dedication to her work and, frankly, was proud of the strides she had made. But today, something felt off.

He glanced at his phone again. Still no messages from her. He frowned. It wasn't like Zenya to be out of touch for this long. They had always maintained a tight connection, especially given their shared interests in groundbreaking technology. Usually, she would send a quick text or make a call when she was busy or caught up in something. But there had been nothing. No "I'm tied up in a meeting" or "Can't talk right now" messages—just silence.

His fingers hovered over his screen for a moment before he dialed her number. The phone rang once, twice, three times. No answer. He furrowed his brow and hung up. Something wasn't right.

He checked the time—an hour had passed since he had sent the first text. His gut twisted in unease. This wasn't like Zenya at all. She was always on top of things, always quick to respond, even if it was just a short acknowledgment. He knew her well enough to sense when something was amiss, and right now, everything felt wrong. He tried again. Dialing her number once more, the ringing tone seemed endless. His anxiety grew.

After a few more unsuccessful attempts, McAdams stood up, pacing the room. He ran a hand through his hair, a mixture of frustration and genuine concern building up inside him. Where could she be? The thought crossed his mind that maybe she was wrapped up in one of her projects or trapped in a meeting she couldn't escape from, but the truth was, this kind of silence from Zenya was deeply unsettling. They had been close for years—he knew her habits, her routine, and most importantly, her safety protocols. She wasn't the type to ignore calls, especially when things were getting critical in her line of work.

A cold shiver ran down his spine as he thought of the recent articles he'd read about the risks surrounding cloning and genetic experimentation in Florida. The very technologies Zenya had been so heavily involved in, the ones that promised revolutionary breakthroughs, also carried with them a host of dangers. Unregulated research, rogue scientists, corporate greed—anything could go wrong in such a high-stakes environment. But that wasn't even what worried him the most. What if someone had found out about Zenya's involvement in this cutting-edge research? What if her discoveries had made her a target?

His mind raced with worst-case scenarios. He tried to shake them off, but the worry lingered. He reached for his phone again, this time scrolling through his contacts to find someone who might know where Zenya was. He called a few of their mutual friends—no one had heard from her. He called her colleagues at the lab, but the response was the same: no one had seen her.

McAdams felt a knot tighten in his chest. He couldn't just sit around waiting for Zenya to call him back. It had already been too long. His mind was made up. He needed to take action. He grabbed his jacket, his heart pounding in his ears as he threw on his shoes. It was time to find her. The streets of the city were bustling with people, but McAdams wasn't focused on anything except one thing: Zenya.

He had known her long enough to understand that if she were in any kind of danger, she wouldn't make a scene. She wasn't someone to call for help unless it was absolutely necessary. This was someone who had spent years conducting sensitive research, often alone in a lab or deep in a project that no one could fully comprehend. McAdams knew that Zenya wasn't the type to panic, but now, he couldn't help but feel that panic rising in him.

His phone buzzed. McAdams snatched it up, hoping it was a message from Zenya. It wasn't. It was from a mutual friend of theirs, asking if he had heard from her. The message sent a chill down McAdams' spine. "I've been trying to reach her all day," the text read. "Have you heard anything? I'm starting to get worried."

That was it. His mind made up, McAdams quickly made his way to the building where Zenya had been working for the past several months. As he approached the entrance, he could feel the tension mounting. He had tried to stay calm, tried to tell himself that maybe she was just caught up in something, but now he wasn't so sure.

The elevator ride to her floor felt like it took forever. Each passing second was agonizing. The silence of the hallway outside her office was almost suffocating. He knocked on her door, but there was no answer. His heart raced faster now, panic taking over. He tried the door handle—it was unlocked. With a deep breath, he pushed the door open, stepping into the dimly lit room. The office was empty. Her desk was in disarray, papers scattered, but there were no signs of struggle.

McAdams' heart sank. Where was she?

He dialed her number one last time, his fingers trembling. This time, the call went through. But it wasn't Zenya who answered.

"Hello?" A strange voice responded.

"Who is this?" McAdams' voice was low, tense.

The voice on the other end paused before responding, "She's... not available right now."

The line went dead.

Cloning in Broward County: A Look at the Present and Future of Scientific Innovation

Cloning, once relegated to the realm of science fiction, has made significant strides into the world of reality, transforming the fields of biotechnology, medicine, and even ethics. In places like Broward County, Florida, a hub of research and technological innovation, cloning research has the potential to revolutionize the medical landscape, offering new solutions to age-old problems. While many are familiar with the concept of cloning through popular media, the practical and ethical implications of cloning are complex and multifaceted.

The Rise of Cloning Research in Broward County

Broward County, with its rich mix of diverse communities, top-tier universities, and health centers, has become a focal point for scientific research and innovation in Florida. As of late, several cutting-edge biotech startups, in collaboration with institutions like the University of Miami and Nova Southeastern University, have begun to explore the potential of cloning technologies.

One of the most prominent developments in Broward County has been the establishment of cloning research programs in local biotech companies and academic institutions. These research efforts focus primarily on the biomedical applications of cloning, including stem cell therapy, organ regeneration, and even the potential for human cloning in the future. While human cloning remains a contentious issue globally, the use of cloning techniques in medical treatments and the growing field of therapeutic cloning is becoming a focal point for many researchers in Broward County.

Therapeutic Cloning: The Potential for Regenerative Medicine

Therapeutic cloning, often referred to as somatic cell nuclear transfer (SCNT), involves the creation of an embryo using a person's own cells to generate stem cells that can potentially replace damaged or diseased tissues. This process allows for the generation of tissues or organs that are genetically identical to the patient, which greatly reduces the risk of rejection by the immune system. While the idea may sound futuristic, Broward County researchers have already made significant progress in this area.

Broward's biotech companies have been collaborating with universities and hospitals to develop methods for using cloned cells to treat conditions such as Parkinson's disease, spinal cord injuries, and heart disease. Stem cell research, in particular, is a focus of many of these projects. Stem cells derived from cloned embryos could be used to create replacement tissues or even organs, offering a potential solution to the growing problem of organ shortages.

Additionally, therapeutic cloning could hold the key to curing degenerative diseases. For example, using cloned stem cells, scientists could grow healthy neurons to replace the damaged ones in Parkinson's patients, potentially alleviating the symptoms of the disease and providing hope to millions who suffer from it. Similarly, spinal cord injuries could benefit from the use of cloned cells to repair nerve damage and restore mobility to patients who might otherwise have been left paralyzed for life.

Ethical Considerations: The Debate Over Human Cloning

Despite the promise of therapeutic cloning, the practice is not without its ethical controversies. One of the major concerns surrounding cloning research in Broward County, and globally, is the issue of human cloning. While researchers are focused primarily on the potential medical benefits, the ethical implications of cloning human beings remain a point of intense debate.

Many opponents of human cloning argue that it crosses a moral line, suggesting that cloning could lead to the commodification of human life. Concerns about the possibility of cloning for purposes such as creating genetically modified children, or the potential for cloning to be used in exploitative ways, have prompted legal restrictions in many countries, including the United States. As of now, human cloning is banned in most parts of the country, but the advancements in cloning technology raise the question of whether this ban will hold in the face of continued scientific progress.

In Broward County, debates surrounding the ethical use of cloning have sparked community discussions. Local citizens, ethicists, and religious groups have expressed concerns about the boundaries that need to be established in order to prevent abuses of cloning technology. In response to these concerns, some of the local research initiatives in Broward County have focused exclusively on therapeutic cloning rather than reproductive cloning, emphasizing the medical benefits without delving into the more contentious aspects of the practice.

The Future of Cloning in Broward County: Medical Applications and Beyond

While Broward County has made significant strides in therapeutic cloning, the future of cloning in the area is far from set in stone. As technology continues to evolve, it is possible that the uses of cloning will expand into areas such as agricultural cloning and even the preservation of endangered species.

In the agricultural sector, cloning could be used to improve livestock production, particularly in the context of cloning animals with desirable traits such as disease resistance or improved meat quality. Broward County's thriving agricultural industry could potentially benefit from the ability to clone high-performing livestock, leading to greater food security and efficiency in the production of animal-based products.

Moreover, cloning may play an increasingly important role in the conservation of endangered species. As biodiversity declines around the world, the ability to clone endangered animals could offer a lifeline for species at risk of extinction. Local research programs in Broward County, in collaboration with wildlife conservation organizations, could eventually lead to the development of cloning methods to preserve the genetic diversity of endangered species, offering hope for a future where at-risk animals are given a fighting chance for survival.

The Role of Public Perception and Policy

The role of public perception and policy cannot be understated in shaping the future of cloning in Broward County. As cloning research progresses, it will be essential for local policymakers to strike a balance between encouraging scientific innovation and addressing public concerns about the ethical implications of cloning technologies. Additionally, the general public will play a crucial role in determining how these technologies are implemented, as well as what regulations should be put in place to ensure that cloning research is conducted responsibly.

Public outreach, educational initiatives, and open discussions will be vital in ensuring that the people of Broward County are fully informed about the potential benefits and risks of cloning technologies. Only through transparency and dialogue can society reach a consensus on how cloning should be approached and regulated.

Conclusion

Cloning in Broward County represents both a remarkable opportunity and a complex challenge. With its focus on therapeutic applications, ethical considerations, and potential future advancements in the field, cloning research in the area is poised to reshape the future of medicine, agriculture, and conservation. As Broward County continues to make strides in the science of cloning, it is crucial for the community to engage in thoughtful discussions and decision-making processes that will guide the responsible use of these technologies. The potential for cloning to improve lives is undeniable, but its ethical complexities must be carefully navigated to ensure that the future of cloning is one that benefits all of humanity.

CHAPTER 28

The Final Chapter: The 3-0161 Gene Experiment
The End of Zhang Legacy

As Victoria stood at the heart of the Infinity estate, surrounded by holograms, secrets, and a past she was only beginning to understand, the weight of her decision became impossible to ignore. A flashback from a year ago in the Hamptons filled her mind—*the Northern lights shimmering across the sky,* a surreal reminder of the crossroads she now faced. Space, her destiny, or the unknown future on Earth—this was the moment that would change everything.

A single question lingered in her mind as the camera scanned her iris at the Infinity estate's gates: *Would she step into a new chapter of human evolution, or would she remain anchored to a planet teetering on the edge of collapse?*

At the meeting, the weight of her father's legacy, her family's involvement in the secret society, and the looming presence of the Zhang family coalesced into a singular, earth-shattering moment. As the hologram of her father, Carlos, materialized before her eyes, she couldn't shake the eerie familiarity of his presence. *He was here, but he wasn't.*

"Victoria," her father's voice crackled through the air, "if you are at Infinity, do not be frightened. My beautiful daughter, I am with you, always. Now, the time has come to make your choice."

It was too much. The hologram, the legacy, the families' secret agendas—it was overwhelming. But as the truth about the cloning process unfolded, revealing the dire need for her to continue the Zhang and DeRossi legacy in space, her heart began to race. *This wasn't just about cloning—it was about saving Earth, saving humanity from its own extinction.*

Phil's words hung in the air like a cold, unrelenting fog. "You are the chosen one, Victoria. The shareholders have selected you. We need you to continue the legacy. But if you decline, you forfeit your right to Infinity. You will be left behind."

The final push came when Phil opened the second panel. It wasn't just a brochure—it was the culmination of years of research, secrets, and endless sacrifices. The *3-0161 gene experiment* was not just a method of cloning. It was the key to unlocking eternal life. It was the portal to humanity's new existence. And it lay in her hands.

As the interactive glass display lit up, showing real-time footage of planets being formed, Victoria's resolve solidified. She saw it—the crystalized stars, the galaxy expanding faster than anyone had ever dared to imagine. A new world was waiting. The Earth's demise was inevitable. But space... Space was a new beginning.

A deep, resonant voice echoed through the room, pulling her focus back to the task at hand. *The alien appeared.*

A massive, eight-foot-tall being, its greenish skin shimmering with an unnatural glow, stepped into the room. Though it spoke without words, its message was clear—*this was the future.* Victoria's pulse quickened as the alien's telepathic communication filled her mind.

"Victoria do not be afraid," the voice inside her head said, like the echo of a dream. "I am here to guide you. Your journey in space is inevitable. Your father's dream is about to become a reality. The 3-0161 gene experiment is the next step for humanity. But only you can decide its fate."

In the distance, a soft hum began to fill the room. It was like the very fabric of the universe was aligning. The tension in the room thickened, and just as the alien's words faded into her thoughts, a live feed appeared on the table. The planets, the galaxies, the immense expanse of space, all streamed before her eyes, ready for her command.

As her fingers hovered over the final panel, Victoria took a deep breath. This wasn't just about her father, or the Zhang family — it was about the future of Earth, the future of humanity, and her place among the stars.

"I'm ready," she whispered, knowing this was more than a decision—it was a leap into the unknown.

The room erupted in a soft golden glow. Phil, Yuan, and the rest of the Zhang family stood by her, their expressions filled with anticipation. *Her time had come.*

The final decision was made.

In an instant, Victoria's hand moved to the panel, activating the hologram and beginning the countdown for the launch. She felt a surge of energy as the holograms flickered, and the space around her shimmered, as if the universe itself had just opened its arms to embrace her.

"Welcome to your new reality, Victoria," Phil said, his voice thick with admiration. "Your father's dream is alive. And now, it is yours."

With a final glance at the Earth, she felt herself drawn upwards—toward the stars, toward space. A ship waited for her, ready to take her beyond the boundaries of Earth's crumbling future.

The countdown clock on the display blinked to light, *T-minus 10 seconds.*

As the room filled with the sounds of the final moments, the stars above began to twinkle, reflecting the promise of a new beginning. The space station loomed in the distance, just beyond the horizon of Earth, and with a final, heart-pounding breath, Victoria's hand rested against the control panel.

3... 2... 1...

And then, in an explosion of light and sound, she was gone—launched into the unknown, leaving Earth behind.

The screen went black, and the final words flashed across the screen:

To be continued in *Infinity*...

INFINITY

Sequel to Zhang Legacy Trilogy Book 2 of 3

Get ready for the most mind-blowing ride yet! **Infinity** is just the beginning, and the stakes are higher than ever as we dive deeper into the secrets of the *Zhang Legacy* trilogy. Fans of the series have been waiting for this moment, and it's finally here. The secrets behind the Southampton estate, the enigmatic Geonomics Cloning team, and Dr. Richard Slate III are about to come to light in ways you won't believe.

Infinity will set the stage for a new world of space tourism, where the unthinkable happens—it's no longer just for the ultra-wealthy 1%. Space travel is opening up to the masses, and what lies beyond the stars will redefine humanity's future. Prepare to embark on a journey to a new golden world— **Beyond Infinity**, where adventure, mystery, and breathtaking discoveries await.

And here's the best part: **Infinity** is not just the next chapter in this gripping saga, but it's also coming soon to a screen near you. Get ready to experience this epic journey in a whole new way with a TV series adaptation that will leave you on the edge of your seat!

But that's not all—the final book in the trilogy, currently untitled, is scheduled for release in **mid-December 2025**, and it will blow your mind. The conclusion to this epic saga is going to leave you questioning everything you thought you knew. As secrets unfold, space tourism takes a revolutionary turn, and the characters you've come to love—and love to question—will face their most shocking revelations yet.

So buckle up, because **Infinity** is just the beginning. The **Zhang Legacy** trilogy is about to take you to places you've only dreamed of, and you won't want to miss a second of it. Get ready for a thrilling conclusion that will leave you breathless, and prepare to journey into a world where the stars are no longer the limit. This is a golden age beyond Infinity, and it's only getting started.

ABOUT THE AUTHOR

Wendy Cottiers is the acclaimed author who coined the term "GMO-Disease" in her debut work. Her wellness philosophy, encapsulated in the book *Healthy is Not a Size; It's a Lifestyle*, was featured onboard the MSC Divina, the world's premier Italian luxury liner, as part of the *Holistic Holiday at Sea* program.

A native of Manhattan, Wendy now resides in South Florida, where she enjoys the vibrant local culture, while spending her summers in the Hamptons. Her early love for storytelling began in her childhood, when she wrote short skits that involved her entire family performing them in the backyard of their Gerritsen Beach home in Brooklyn, New York. It was in this same neighborhood that she learned to swim at Kiddie Beach. In 1980, her family relocated to Florida, and she grew up in the rapidly developing city of Coral Springs.

Zhang Legacy marks Wendy Cottiers' debut novel, which has since been translated into ten languages and is available in audiobook. The idea for the book came to Wendy in a vivid dream featuring a Xian Warrior who saved a young girl from a catastrophic mega-tsunami. Inspired by this vision, she crafted the draft for Chapter 5 of the book, which eventually became the cornerstone of the novel.

Infinity, the highly anticipated sequel, will be released on Valentine's Day 2025. The final installment of the trilogy is scheduled for release in December 2025. For updates on book signings and Cottiers' Heart Healthy Retreats, please visit www.wendycottiers.com and follow Wendy on Instagram @Wendy_CottiersAuthor.